THE GABBIN

A Middle Earth Parody

The Lad of the Rings: Book 1

By: Johann Balthasar Knörtzer

The Gabbin

Copyright © 2021 by Johann Balthasar Knörtzer

This book is a work of fiction. Names, characters, businesses, organizations, places, events, and incidents either are the product of the author's imagination or are used fictitiously. Any resemblance to actual persons, living or dead, events, or locales is entirely coincidental.

For more information, or to contact us, visit:
https://www.mythicbooksboutique.com/johanns-blog

Book and Cover design by
Johann Knörtzer and Roberta Knörtzer

Paperback ISBN: 9781954948006
Hardcover ISBN: 9781954948013
E-book ISBN: 9781954948020

First Edition: March 2021

10 9 8 7 6 5 4 3 2

V.9

Dedication

For my son and daughter;

for my wife who took on the challenge of organizing, editing, and pushing me to continue writing;

for my friend, cousin, and contributor Eddockelino Meriodon Knörtzer, without whom this story would have never existed;

and for the handful of friends and family who were interested in seeing the short, fragmented tale that sat lost and abandoned in computer files since 2005 be brought into an expanded and finalized physical book.

Table of Contents

Prologue:
History

Long ago, in the land of Skiddle Earth, a glorious tree was planted. The tree was so magical, that only the very strongest could go near it, for it would destroy all who lacked the strength of body and mind to withstand its incredible power. It was the most perfect of all growing things in the world, for it was indeed an apple tree, yet it produced extraordinarily shiny oranges. The people of the lands foolishly gave all their money to the tree in respect to its power, until it led them to their ruin. Wars were waged and empires collapsed as the kingdoms of the world fought to the brink of extinction for the favor of its branchy magnificence.

Almost five hundred years after the planting of the tree, a prince was born. He grew to become the mightiest of all men in the lands, which made him proud and arrogant. The people loved him despite this, but one day, he decided that he shouldn't just be prince of Skiddle Earth, he should be king. He murdered up his parents and blamed it on innocent men, who were put to death... twice.

After that, he took the sacred Aplornge tree and moved it to a faraway place. With the tree gone, everyone followed him without question. The new king eventually became so great, admired, and influential, especially to the most powerful leaders in the surrounding kingdoms, that he made twenty-eight rings with which these lower rulers could now better govern their respective lands using the magical properties contained within them.

Some gave extended life, increased physical strength, and enhanced abilities of the mind. Others gave more outlandish gifts, such as rubbery limbs, x-ray hearing, a nose that grew in length in accordance with how much gold the wearer possessed, and one that made the wearer invincible to baldness. After the king gave them all out, he made two more for himself. None suspected he had done so, due to his making them while no one was looking. To make it even more convincing, he had the words, 'I Certainly Only Made Twenty-Eight Rings, Not Thirty', embroidered in large, bold, italic, underlined letters upon the back of his silken robes.

The rings that he certainly *did* make, however, were powerful rings indeed, with which he could control all life in Skiddle Earth through the lesser power of the twenty-eight. One was the Ring of the Time, and the other was the Ring of the Phone. As the writers of old would come to say:

THE GABBIN

Ten Rings for the Elvish kings in the dry,
Ten for the Dork-Lords with their walls and thrones,
Five for the distorted men doomed to cry,
and Three for the Wents with twigs for bones,
in the land of Dormor where Dragons fly;
Two Rings to control them all,
Two Rings to hide them,
Two Rings to drink them all,
and in the carpets grind them,
in the land of Dormor where Dragons fly.

This was how the king, now known as The Dark King Rauson, would take over the entire world and bend it to his own selfish purposes.

When the nations and peoples of Men, Elves, Dorks, and Wents eventually realized what Rauson's plan was, they set aside their differences and charged the treacherous king's armies at the base of Mount Zoom in his fortress of Dormor. When they thought they had killed the majority of his evil Porks, The Dark King himself came forth with the power of the Two Rings. He easily and single-handedly cut through the opposing armies like hot cheese... the rings were just too powerful. The hearts of the free people began to falter, and many turned to flee. Yet from amongst the vast host of that great resistance, The King of Men stepped forth and challenged Rauson alone. The king did all that he could, and mighty he was, but alas he was not strong enough. He got whacked by Rauson and fell to the ground in complete and total death.

The remaining forces rallied together again at the sight of the fallen hero, and in a final charge they backed Rauson up, all the way into the cave of Mount Zoom where the rings were made. Then Durisil, son of The King of Men, took his father's pitchfork and cut the Ring of the Time from Rauson's wretched hand. Then the dark king was knocked backward into the lake of extreme cold... the waters of Zoom. He had been defeated, and the Ring of the Phone was destroyed. Durisil then took the Ring of the Time for his own and sold it.

Shortly after, he had his teeth kicked out by bandits on the road. He was never seen again... except by dead people. The ring ended up in a shop, where Jeegle, a fellow from the creek villages bought it. It made him go crazy and he ran into the Mimson Mountain caverns. He loved the ring more than anything, and for ages it controlled him. Yet unbeknownst to him, a day would come when a little fat man would find his ring and take it from him. This is the account of Bobill Gabbin, Mayor of Hometown, and his adventurous discovery of a mysterious and particularly special rounded object....

Chapter 1:
A Wizard Visits

There was once a man who lived under a pile of mud. His name was Bobill Gabbin. He didn't care for adventures or anything of such fashion. His interest was in the town of Hometown, collecting worthless crap, and playing the fiddle; not at all of the things in the outside world. It should be noted that he was the mayor of the town as well... although he really wasn't. You see, he liked to complain often, it being another of his favorite hobbies.

So, one day he formed a group, that nobody else in the town joined, to elect someone as a leader to address the issues within the town. When it came time for the election, he had set up everything himself, and he was the only one that voted. Without anyone else in the town ever knowing, he was secretly the self-proclaimed mayor of Hometown, and he held that title with high honor all of his days.

Now as far his appearance went, this much can be said: his hair was a peppery-yellow winter brown color with some mild curling to it, his eyes were just little black dots, and he was rather short, as were the rest of the folk in his country. He was also fat and liked to stuff his chubby cheeks with cakes and sweets. As a matter of fact, he ate twelve meals a day, one every hour. He *would* eat twenty-four if he wasn't forced to sleep. Which he did for twelve hours also. So far in his life, the most amazing thing he had ever done was say hello to someone that he was not sure lived in his town. But very soon, he would find himself doing things more interesting than that.

One evening, as Bobill poured a cup of triple-sugar tea from his favorite brass kettle and was about to open the oven to fetch his fifth batch of frosted buttercake muffins, he heard a rather large knock on his front door. He tossed his apron on a chair and scurried to the door to answer it.

He slowly opened it and said in a rather frightened voice, "H-h-h-hello?"

Lightning flashed, and Bobill saw a creepy old man sporting a long yellowish beard and a tall pointy dark yellow hat. He was holding a crooked staff and standing in his doorway glaring down at him.

"Sakes!" screamed Bobill.

"I am a Wizard by the name of Randolf the Bronze," said the Wizard named Randolf the Bronze. "I am here on important business that is none of your business. Just let me in, let me have some of those frosted buttercake muffins, and let us talk."

Bobill nearly passed out, but he straightened himself up and found the courage to say, "Well of course, my good Wizard, always a pleasure to serve a senior citizen."

Randolf, stepping in the doorway, slipped on some mud on the floor and cracked his head of bronze on a cheese grater.

"My goodness, Randolf!" exclaimed Bobill. "I'm sorry about that."

Randolf slapped Bobill's hand away when he tried to help him up and jumped up quicker than he fell. He then proceeded to dust off his brazen kilt and sat down at Bobill's little table. As he tossed the first muffin in his pie-hole, he asked Bobill a very certain question. This question of certainty upset Bobill and put him in a rebellious mood. The question proposed to Bobill was one that dealt with taking an adventure into the outside world.

"Would you be willing, young Bobill, to journey to faraway lands and kill Dragons and Porks and other unspeakable things?"

Bobill was frozen with fear and began to sob loudly.

Randolf knew that he was quite unwelcome there now, so he got up, grabbed his hat and staff, and left Bobill's home. Once Bobill was sure he had left, he instantly cracked a large grin.

"Fooled that old codger I did!" he laughed.

He giggled to himself into the night, shaking his head every time he thought of how clever he was.

The very next morning Randolf came back. Bobill was extra frustrated when he heard the knocking on his door at this hour. He ran all over the house making sure everything was perfect before he dared even go see who it was... although he had a pretty good guess. He then went over and slowly opened the door. Bobill had guessed correctly, but to his surprise, there were six Dorks with the Wizard this time. Of course, he had never seen a real Dork before. He had never even been outside of his town. But from what he had heard and read in his books, these short, wide, bearded fellows must almost certainly be genuine Dorks. Letting them in was the last thing he wanted to do.

"Come in! Welcome!" said Bobill with a frown.

Randolf strutted in, minding the slick entryway this time, as the six Dorks ran in past him and started smashing things and throwing Bobill's pictures and trophies for doing who knows what all over the place.

"AHHHH!!" screamed Bobill. "What are they doing!?"

Randolf replied, "They are searching, they have to make sure you aren't some fool."

The Dorks looked at each other and nodded, then they lined up in front of Bobill.

Randolf pointed to each one. "This is Porky, Jerky, Corky, Slerky, Dorky, and Forky Rottenfield, their leader."

Then they all said together in a kind of frightful voice, "We are all at your servings, Bobill!"

So, he felt obligated to make them some dinner. Bobill feared he would have nothing left for himself after emptying out his mud cupboards of food supplies for cooking. The Dorks ate like a pack of wild fatties. Gulping, slurping, crunching, munching, devouring, and inhaling everything that Bobill put on the table as fast as he could cook it. On at least two occasions his fingertips were bitten.

That night, the Dorks had eaten six roast turkeys, four fried hams, twenty-three fish tacos, thirty-two ears of corn, a baker's dozen of potatoes, four 7.3-pound cheddar cheese wheels, threescore of sprinkled donuts, twelve cantaloafes, five bushels of purpaberries, two beans, a frozen block of gravy, sixteen dozen eggs cooked and prepared in all possible forms, and finally, an innumerable amount of

Bobill's prized buttercakes. Randolf ate his own small portion from all this, but Bobill, left with nothing but a barren pantry, had to make do with a tiny bag of unflavored powdered pudding mix.

After they had all finished their dinner, they moved to the living room to discuss some sort of business associated with their leader Forky. Bobill pretended to be uninterested, and he certainly was, but he couldn't help overhearing some of it from the other room while he was still sweeping up shards of his vaporized platery. Evidently, the Dorks were to cross through the country, all the way to the distant Mountain of Solitude. Once there, they required somebody's special talents to sneak in the back way of the mountain and get some of Forky's gold that was being kept from him. Bobill was distressed about this, especially when he realized who that somebody was. They were talking like Bobill would be accompanying them on their nonsensical trip.

"I suppose that's what Randolf was rambling about yesterday," thought Bobill. *"Well, aren't they in for a real letdown!"*

He had already had quite enough of Dorks for a lifetime. Besides, he really had no skills other than allowing others to take advantage of him, so he would certainly not be going anywhere. He didn't ever want to leave his quiet mudhole, for he was quite content there. It was a laughable notion, and it absolutely wasn't happening, no matter what anyone said.

Eventually, he decided to leave with them. Bobill sat down while Forky and his Dorks explained in great vagueness the journey they would be taking. He was made to sign an uninteresting document that he briefly scanned over, noting short phrases such as 'certain death' and an absurdly high number of instances of the word 'probably'. As he signed his name, Bobill envisioned himself visiting some wondrous locations, and possibly even coming back with enough cash to restock his pantry. Maybe getting out of the house for a change wouldn't be so bad, and he'd be better off for it.

"And that is that," said Forky, crumpling up the paper. "Welcome to our humble crew, Mister Gabbin."

Randolf then told them all to get some rest since they would be starting early in the morning. Bobill grabbed all the extra pillows and blankets he could find to make the Dorks comfortable. Then, when he was sure everyone had what they needed, he put all the lights out, went back to his own bed, and flopped down on it, quite surprised that it hadn't been taken. Suddenly, the Dorks got out their trumpets and drums and started slamming out a tune. It was going to be a long night for Bobill.

When Bobill awoke and came out of his bedroom, he

was shocked to find the Dorks were gone.

"Thank goodness!" he cried. "What an idiot I was for saying I'd go on that stupid journey. My place is here, not wandering in some crazy far-off lands!"

He sat down at his dining room table, sighing in relief.

Out of nowhere, a rough whispery voice came from unseen lips that were mere inches from his ear. "They'll be back any moment now, went into town to grab some fresh supplies."

It was Randolf, who had apparently not left. Bobill was still clutching his chest and hyperventilating when the Dorks kicked the front door in. They allowed him just enough time to recover and grab a few of his belongings before they dragged him out the door.

Chapter 2:
The Journey Starts Up

Bobill, the six Dorks, and Randolf were marching through Hometown with their knees flying high above their heads, but as they grew closer to the border of Hometown, Bobill became more and more unwilling to continue on. As he stood there not wanting to go any further, he suddenly fell to the ground and his body began to slide rapidly. Corky the Dork had grabbed him and was now dragging him again. After a couple of his favorite white teeth were chipped on the gravel, Bobill decided that he would rather walk than be dragged on the unforgiving ground.

"Get off me!" yelled Bobill.

"*Here we go to and fro, to the hills where grass don't grow...*" the Dorks were singing.

"Hey! Listen to me!!" Bobill screamed. "GET OFF OF ME!!!"

"*...To the hills where grass don't g...*" the Dorks stopped singing and looked at Bobill.

"What's wrong?" Corky asked.

"WILL YOU PLEASE LET ME GO!?" Bobill had just about lost his temper.

Immediately, they turned around and continued singing and marching down the old dusty road. Bobill, still being drug by Corky, couldn't take it anymore, so he started smacking Corky's hand quickly until he finally let go. Even so, Corky never flinched and kept on singing with the rest of the Dorks. Meanwhile, Randolf was far ahead of the group and paying no heed to Bobill's suffering. The Dorks' singing was starting to get to Bobill. He thought he was going to go mad. He was just about ready to turn and sprint back to his home as fast as his short legs would carry him.

After a while, for some reason, the Dorks actually stopped for a moment, and Bobill was very relieved. He saw that they were unpacking their instruments. Then on they sang, while not playing anything even resembling music along with it...

"With cheese in the dirt,
and dirt in our hair,
and hair on our toes,
we are very fair,
hair ev'rywhere, hair ev'rywhere, hair everywheeeerrreee!!

THE GABBIN

Through the valleys and over the mountains,
we sing this song and drink from the fountains!
We march on with our hairy old toes,
and defeating all foes,
from where the grass grows!
We work with cheese,
and we always get fleas,
they make us sneeze,
as we dance in the breeze...
With cheese in the dirt,
and dirt in our hair,
and hair on our toes,
we goes, and goes, and GOES!!!"

FINALLY, after this, they stopped for a while. Bobill managed to calm himself a bit and took in the strange new smells and sights of this land one mile from his home. He realized just then that he could do it. He could do great things if only people would force him to.

Hoping the Dorks were just morning people, Bobill found them to be a bit more pleasant as the day drew on and they began to settle down. He even made some time to walk and speak with each of them and found they were not all exactly the same, as he originally supposed. Forky, the leader, was the tallest by an eighth of a millimeter, had a rough black beard, blackened hair shaped like that of swirled ice-cream upon his dome, and was the quickest to irritation. He also tended to display the greatest voice of reason within the group, falling less into the nonsense that the others so readily embraced.

Corky was somewhat of a second in command. He took charge quickly if he heard no word from Forky. He was carefree and heeded not the complaints of others. Though when he felt like it, he could be a slightly helpful fellow. He was certainly a little more on the round side, had a wide corn-blonde beard, and what hair he possessed was concealed under a red pointy hat.

Now Jerky could come off as rude, but he was actually only like that *most* of the time. He kept to himself often but offered many a quick sarcastic remark when he felt it necessary. The Dork was a crack shot at axe-throwing and was known to take out birds on the wing at a moment's notice. At least that's what Bobill heard anyway. Jerky kept his graying comb-over under a dark hood at nearly all times, his equally gray beard could normally be found split in twain and tied at the ends. It was usually the only thing to be seen poking out from his hood, aside from a lengthy nose.

Dorky wasn't the most coordinated and had trouble with many simple tasks. However, it didn't stop him from excelling at a few things, such as organizing items in their packs, overabundant memorization of useless facts, and knowing how to steam a pair of slacks. The top of his head was adorned with curls of crimson-brown, and his narrow reddish beard was often tied in one big knot.

The next Dork, Slerky, was a bit strange and quiet. He spoke almost exclusively in whispery mumbling gibberish unless he had something important to say. He could be cheerful and sing as foolishly loud as the others at times but didn't stay that way long. He was one of the few Dorks who dared wield a bow, for many of their kind believed it to be a weapon for different and unlikeable folk with pointy ears. He wore a triangular, feathered, green hat which sat upon his shoulder-length, wavy, brown hair. His darker brown beard was a prosthetic, though he was never known to take it off. His original had been blown off in a tragic blasting accident, years ago when he was still mining the tunnels under the great halls of the Dork-Lords.

The last of them, Porky, had a brown beard as well, though lighter than Slerky's fake one. It was kept in three thick parallel braids, and each braid held tight a different utensil: a fork, a spoon, and a knife. He wore a tall black cooking pot on his balding head, and upon the hilt of his axe that doubled as a spatula, was fastened a ladle. The Dork was easily the size of any two and a half of the others, yet he seemed to have no trouble keeping up their pace. He had considerable knowledge of edible things and knew how to cook up nearly anything.

Now that Bobill was more acquainted with his party, he felt much better about moving on and not running home screaming. He figured they weren't as bad as he originally thought them to be, though still quite annoying. As long as they kept their singing to a minimum and quit trying to drag his face on the ground, things might be alright.

They continued down the road with Randolf and Forky at the head of the pack. The last houses of Bobill's town had long faded into the distance behind them.

Just then, Randolf yelled back to everyone, "We are crossing the borders of Hometown. Mister Gabbin, do not expect to find cakes and tea in the unbelievable wilderness!"

Bobill did notice that he hadn't eaten in an hour and a half. So, he pulled out a cheese-log with almonds and oats on top and began to munch. Dorky glanced back and saw Bobill's treat, and though he had food of his own, he coveted it.

He pointed behind Bobill and screamed, "It's Rauson!"

Bobill looked back and said, "Who the heck is—"

He turned back around just in time to see Dorky licking his fingers, and his own hands were straight empty.

"Uugghh!!" Bobill complained.

He looked around for Randolf to whine to him, but quickly discovered he had vanished.

"Where did Randolf go?" he asked.

Forky's large eyes shot back to Bobill, and he replied, "He's a Wizard, my dear Gabbin. It's what he does. He appears and disappears frequently. Who knows why? Though we're pretty sure we've seen him hiding behind trees nearby, only to show up later out of breath and going on about amazing adventures he just went on."

Bobill frowned. Since the food was strictly rationed, he would go hungry for now, but not nearly as hungry as later on in this story you're currently reading.

On through the evening they hiked, putting twenty-five miles between them and Bobill's cozy home. The group had consumed everything they brought with them by this time and began to search for something to eat.

As night began to fall, Corky pointed to an area off the side of the road and whispered, "There's a large campfire just through those trees. Let's move closer and take a look-see!"

So, they crept through the brush and around the thick trees, careful to be silent and not alert whoever or whatever was utilizing the fire. When they got close enough, they peered their faces out from the bushes and could see now just what it was. In a semi-circle on the far side of the flames, four Trolls were sitting down and eating a large amount of roast buttons.

Forky whispered, "Hey, Gabbin! Go on over and get us some of those buttons!"

Chapter 3:
Roast Buttons

Bobill, after a bit of whining, cut wide around the Trolls' campfire clearing, snuck up behind them, and tried to steal some of their dinner. He was extremely afraid of getting too close to them though. So, he sat crouched behind one of their large lawn chairs in the dark for a moment.

Now Trolls are known to be arguitous, and Bobill had heard about this long ago. He thought he might wait until their arguing was at its most intense (which happened about every twenty minutes) before he swiped those delicious buttons. It was soon obvious what their names were, since they were constantly screaming them in each other's faces along with large amounts of saliva.

The largest and most ferocious was Grickleton, who had several horns on his head, and looked like he may have had something in his left eye (it was red). To his right (clockwise) was Berp. Somewhat short for a Troll, and fatter than his mother the day she gave birth to him and his nine siblings simultaneously. The next Troll's name was Greg, quieter and calmer than the others, and quite thin. Finally, the most normal-looking Troll was Rugbin. He was so average that there isn't much to describe.

Their arguing was quickly escalating. With Berp yelling that he was jealous of Rugbin and Grickleton's larger mouths that could intake more food at a time. Greg was complaining about how they always argue. Grickleton was always angry at everything and would swing large logs at the other Troll's faces periodically, which set them to arguing. Rugbin was mad that all they ever ate was buttons.

"Button cereal, button sammiches, button stew... I'm sick of 'em!" he yelled. "Button chips, buttoncakes, button steaks..." his voice trailed off, but he continued grumbling.

Greg stuck his fingers in his earholes and was continuously screaming, "SHUT UP! SHUT UP! SHUT UP!"

Berp was still going on about mouth sizes. "I say you two have the right scale eat-holes. Mine is so small, that I nearly starve to death even while I'm eatin'!" He slapped his enormous belly for emphasis, and it did not stop bouncing until later.

Grickleton finally blew his top, ripped a giant tree out of the ground, and swung it across all three of the other Troll's faces.

'Whack-whack-whack!!!' was the sound that night that Bobill *would've* heard if he wasn't fast asleep under Grickleton's lawn chair. He was spotted by one of the Trolls and it grabbed him by the toe.

"I don't know what this is," said the biggest Troll Grickleton, "but I'm gonna eat it!!"

Bobill screamed like a wild goose.

Just as the Troll was about to release his grip and drop Bobill down his gullet, the Dorks ran in and began kicking all of the Trolls' ankles. Bobill flipped out of Grickleton's grasp and did a dive-roll on the ground. A fight began and Bobill and the Dorks quickly lost. The Trolls took them all and hung them by their toes with clothespins in the surrounding trees. None of them could figure out what the Dorks were, much less Bobill. They argued for a while about this, even worse than earlier, and started to get extremely angry with each other.

They yelled things like, "This one's a pig! I'm sure of it!" and "No! They're obviously all turkeys!"

They took so long arguing about what they were, and how they were going to eat them, that they got old and died. It wasn't until one second later that Bobill and the Dorks found out that Randolf was the one that sped up their aging. The Wizard had returned to them... for a while.

Randolf swung out of a tree, did a flip or two in the air, and landed on one knee nearby. His staff was still smoking from the aging magic, so he had to resort to more crude measures of getting Bobill and the Dorks down from their lofty inverted prisons. Randolf removed his hat and threw it like a discus, slicing off every branch that held a member of the group within an inch of their toes. Six 'thuds' and a 'poip' were heard in quick succession as they fell to the ground on their heads.

After Corky and Slerky's hats were straightened and Porky dislodged his cooking pot from the dirt, the Dorks said a mumbly, ungrateful '*thanks*' to Randolf, who seemed annoyed at how easily the Dorks almost died without him there to hold their hands. Bobill however, was more than happy to see the Wizard and thanked him sincerely many times more than was acceptable.

After gathering themselves, the group searched around the campfire for some food and supplies. They ate roast buttons until they nearly popped, and Dorky stuffed what was left into equally divided portions in their packs. The rest of the items there were not of much use to them, for they were enormous in size. They had almost given up looking around and were about to head out again when Jerky called out from nearby. He had found a cave on the other side of the hill behind the campfire.

Everyone came quickly, and after some inspection and determining that it was possibly safe, they made a few torches and were led by Randolf down through the dark opening. Inside, they found what looked like the Trolls' abode. There was a stone couch, some stone beds, and a stone table. In a back corner, sitting high up on a stone shelf above a stone counter was a very large jar. Bobill and Randolf climbed up on to the counter to see what was inside. The Dorks soon followed, and when they had gathered around, Randolf took note of a strange inscription etched into the front of the jar.

'Tuefpix', the jar's label read.

Forky reached forth his axe and knocked the jar onto its side. From the many round holes punched in the top of the jar slid long, sharp objects that gleamed in the torches' light. Swords they were, enough of them for everyone to conveniently have one each. Bobill's sword was actually just a little pocketknife, but he wore it on his belt with much pride. Randolf told him that it was probably made a long time ago and that it may or may not be a quality item. Randolf also took for himself a seemingly valuable sword of silvery splendor. Then Forky sifted through all the ones the rest of the Dorks had taken to make sure his was the nicest.

After they were sure they had gathered everything of any worth, the group made it to the end of the cave and found their way out the far side. When they emerged, they were covered in mud and smelled like pig-poo.

"Something must have died around here you know," said Forky.

"Well, we must move on immediately with haste," quacked Randolf, "but let us first rest here for the remainder of the nightly hours."

So Bobill and the six Dorks threw together some basic beddings and napped in a small grassy clearing. Randolf lodged himself comfortably about sixty feet up in a tree. Bobill slept quite well until Corky and Forky started snoring. It was almost like they were having a contest. One would snore, then the other would snore a little louder, then the other would be a little louder than the last.

This went on until Bobill couldn't take it anymore. He got up from his rest and decided to explore a little. As he neared the cave he and the Dorks had been in earlier, he heard a sound. It was a sound like a terrible monster. Like the worst thing in the world. He tip-toed into the cave a little ways and saw a great beast eating a dead Troll. The beast was easily twice the size of the Troll. Bobill was scared to death, he couldn't even move. He let out a girl-like squeal of fear, and the beast snapped its head around toward him instantly.

Bobill ran the heck out of there and he heard the claws quickly scraping the ground behind him. The growling and heavy breathing were getting closer to the back of his little head. He made it back to the camp, but everyone was gone.

Then, he began to have a pretty serious panic attack and knew his life was coming to a close. He spun around and saw the beast in the air, jaws open. It landed, and clamped down on Bobill... it was over...

THE END

THE GABBIN

Bobill woke up the next day aching from a tree limb that had fallen on his face during the night. Randolf had zapped it off trying to make room to get more comfortable. All that stuff about getting eaten was just a dream. Or was it? Had it really happened? *Had* he been eaten the night before? What are you dumb? Of course not.

Randolf skipped down the limbs of his tree and yelled to the Dorks, "Get up! It's time for us to go to Drivenrail! The land of Elven folk!!"

Everyone packed up their junk and headed out.

Chapter 4:
To Drivenrail & Beyond

After several hours of walking, the journeyers arrived in Drivenrail, and they were all starving. The city was not terribly large, and it was hidden in the woods between a couple of mountains. Actually, one could get quite close and never find it, for it had a majestic magic protecting it from peeping eyes. It also had a bunch of rivers and waterfalls everywhere. The lord of the city was named BellJohn, the Elf who wears one thousand bells on his robes.

He had sent out some of his guards to bring the travelers in and ordered for a great amount of food to be awaiting them upon their arrival. Bobill looked around in wonder at the incredible place as they passed through. Never in his life did he imagine that things could be built so fancily. The smoothly carved stone of the buildings and pillars was bright and seemed to shimmer like sparkly things in the sun. The Dorks rolled their eyes and turned up their noses in forced disgust since they didn't get along well with the fancy Elf people.

THE GABBIN

None of the Dorks truly even knew why they disliked them so much aside from being a bit taller and possibly somewhat easier on the eyes... depending on who you asked.

Randolf stared straight ahead, taking no heed of the beauty that surrounded him, for he had seen this place many times, and finer places besides. But that is a tale you likely won't hear about. The group passed under all sorts of arches and what-have-you, until they came at last to the great front doors. The lower guards that brought them in stepped away as the group came to a couple of slightly extra-fancy Elves that stood guard there. The fancies bowed low before them while rolling a flat hand forth in accordance with their fashion.

Then wordlessly, they quickly turned, grasped the door handles and whipped the great doors open so fast, that Bobill had to grab his head to keep his wig from flying away. Randolf bowed and nodded to the fancies as he took the lead into the grand hall of Drivenrail. There were enormous fireplaces on either side of the room, and between them in the center sat a very long golden table with at least a hundred chairs slid perfectly up under it. The high ceiling over the table held a gigantic chandelier wrought of curving tubelets of golden silver, and from each hung many colorful gems, stones, and gemstones.

On the tops of the tubelets were candles that burned brightly, but never burned out; not even one drip could be found running down the ivory sticklets. If it were by magic or some other Elf-craft this was accomplished, none knew... (except probably the Elves).

"What a tacky-looking shack," said Forky.

Randolf raised his staff at him, shaking it, then pressed a finger to his wizard-lips in warning. Several extremely fancy Elves swished into the room and seated Randolf, Bobill, and the Dorks comfortably near the head of the table. Porky needed two chairs and Bobill required a booster. The food was hot and plentiful before them, and they filled their plates from the countless dishes of edible excellence that lined the middle of the table. They all began to feast hungrily.

"At least it's not MY food this time," thought Bobill, as he choked down some fried ostrich wings.

It was then that BellJohn himself walked in. Slow and graceful his movements were at first, but then, he crouched down and did a backflip, planting his feet firmly into the flat stone above the right-side fireplace mantle. He pushed off hard and extended his limbs outward, each one doing its own strange yet meaningful movements independently, as his body twisted and rolled through the air. Over the chandelier he went, tucking his knees up under him. With one arm he held his knees close, while the other arm waved in circles over his head like he was riding a wild stallion.

He instantaneously switched to three or four more positions all while still sailing over the group's heads. The last was horizontal, legs outstretched and crossed with his right arm draped on his side, and his left supporting his upturned head, propped up on invisible air. He went into a front flip and finally landed on one toe, back facing the table and arms straight. He spun on the toe upon landing, then dropped into another crouch, this time moving and waving his flattened palms all around, then over and between each other. There was a sudden stop of his deadly chopping hands, so quick and violent that the very air in front of him erupted in a loud 'CRACK!'

He held the intimidating and deadly pose for a moment, well-aware of how impressive it was; especially considering the fact that not a single one of the thousand bells attached to his robes made even the slightest sound throughout his entire display.

The only issue was the group at the table had been far too focused on eating to notice anything BellJohn had done. They didn't even know he had come in. BellJohn stood and assumed a more formal stance, then he cleared his throat several times, becoming louder with each one.

Randolf turned his head, and upon seeing BellJohn

there, grabbed his staff and started hitting the rest of his companions' knees under the table while raspily yell-whispering, "Get up you fools! BellJohn, the lord of these halls has arrived!"

Everyone jumped up and bowed except Bobill, who had some wing bones stuck in his throat. He gripped the table and tried with all his might to swallow the bone, but it wouldn't budge. Then he gasped for air and none came. As he looked around the room things began to get blurry. All sounds and feelings faded.

He thought to himself... *"So ends the amazing life of the brave Bobill."*

'SMACK!' Everything came back to him, and he realized Randolf had cracked him in the back with his staff and the bone had flown out and hit BellJohn directly in the face.

"My goodness!" yelled Bobill still looking somewhat pale. "Forgive me, Lord BellJohn!"

BellJohn's extremely fancy servants wiped his face off faster than anyone could blink, and he replied, "You have had a long and hard journey coming here, Mister Gabbin. I will try to forget about this little accident. For now, let us all go into the sitting hall and discuss your travels."

In the sitting hall, in front of another huge fire, Forky and Randolf ran their mouths to BellJohn about the journey so far, and where they intended to go next. BellJohn noticed the weapons at their sides and asked about them. Randolf handed his sword to him, and he studied it. He read the ancient markings upon it and translated them.

"This sword reads: 'Wham-Thing the Jerk Stabber'. It was wielded by a famous king many centuries ago. It is quite the quality item."

Forky handed his to BellJohn as well.

"Ahh, this one translates: 'Porkletz the Pork Carver'. It also belonged to some wonderful person of old."

He handed it back to Forky and happened to see Bobill's knife.

Randolf spoke up. "Mister Gabbin attained a weapon of his own."

Bobill looked down at the floor and shook his head. "No, no I didn't."

BellJohn held out his hand. "Come now, let's have a look."

Bobill swatted BellJohn's hand away and turned the other way whining.

"Mister Gabbin!" yelled Randolf.

BellJohn got irritated and grabbed at the knife. Bobill

gripped the other end of it and they both pulled back and forth. Finally, it slipped out of Bobill's greasy little fingers.

"No! Waah-ha-ha!!" sobbed Bobill.

"Sheesh!" screamed BellJohn. "Anyhow, let us see what the blade says on it. Here it is: 'Stink, the Killer of Meanies'. It poked many an enemy in its day."

As Bobill yanked it back, the rest of the Dorks held out the swords they had found in the Trolls' abode, eagerly awaiting the names and titles of the legendary blades.

BellJohn leaned forward in his seat and looked upon them all at once; then with an eyebrow raised high said, "These are just sharpened sticks painted silver."

The Dorks frowned and backed away. BellJohn stood and clapped his hands two and a half times. In an instant, a few extremely fancy Elf servants were at his sides.

"The day is coming to a close, my friends. You should all certainly get some rest in the sleeping quarters. My servants will show you the way. You will find beds for lying upon in that particular area."

Bobill didn't realize until now how tired he actually was. He, the Dorks and Randolf headed up the stairs into a long hallway. There were many bedrooms for sleeping and each of them got their own room, except for Bobill. Everyone else had run in, slammed their doors, and locked them up tight. Bobill walked up to each one and heard loud snoring inside. Other than the one Randolf was in.

From that door, he heard all sorts of zapping and poofing sounds. Who knows what the Wizard could be doing? But since there were no rooms left, Bobill decided to see if Randolf would share, being the only one still awake. His little fist had barely made the first knock when the door flew open a few inches and stopped. A chain kept it from opening all the way.

A big nose shot out the crack and Randolf yell-whispered to Bobill, "What is it, young Gabbin? Make haste!"

Bobill answered, "There are no rooms left, Randolf, and all the Dorks are fast asleep."

Randolf shoved his hand through the opening right next to his face, closed one eye, and pointed across the hall. As Bobill began to turn around, he heard Randolf's door slam. He looked behind him to find a very small door. He opened it, saw that it was indeed a broom closet, then frowned and walked back over to Randolf's door.

He stood there and listened to a strange sound that went, 'poof-poof-poof!' He threw himself on the floor and peeped under the door. He could barely make out what was going on. Randolf's bed was on fire and Randolf was next to it beating the flames with a pillow. He had been practicing lightning bolts indoors again....

So, Bobill turned around and stuffed himself into the broom closet. It took him a few tries, and of course, he had to remove the cleaning supplies from it, but finally got the door to shut. He eventually drifted off to sleep, standing upright with his face pressed firmly against the door.

Bobill woke up in mid-fall, right before his face smacked the unforgiving floor. 'BAM!' He looked up to see everyone standing over him, packed and ready to go.

"I thought we were staying for a week!" he said, rubbing his poor face.

"It *has* been a week, Bobill," replied Randolf. "We... kind of forgot you were in there. I had a dream that you ran home crying, and since that is so like you to do, I told the Dorks that's what happened."

Bobill rolled his eyes and got up. Then, BellJohn spoke. "My servants have prepared a large breakfast for you all. You can eat as much as you like and take as much as you can carry. Aren't I generous?"

With that, he took his leave and they saw him no more. They went downstairs and ate their fill of toast with jam, cereal, oatmeal, grits, muffins, eggs, sausage, bacon, ham cubes, waffles, pancakes, jamcakes, sweetcakes, cheesecakes, ricecakes, and buttercakes. All they *couldn't* eat, they wrapped up and put into their bags. Moments later, they were all out the door.

Slerky immediately started complaining about how he wanted to stay in Drivenrail. Then Corky joined in. Soon enough, all but Randolf were complaining their heads off about how much nicer it would be to stay there forever.

Randolf yelled at them. "Do you want to go find your treasure or not!?"

Forky yelled back. "It's your fault, Randolf! None of this would have happened if you weren't such a big *Wizard*!"

Randolf smacked him across the face and vanished. Forky came to his senses. It was very difficult to adjust to the outside world once in Drivenrail for so long. They all felt ashamed and had to go on without the Wizard now. A few hours passed of silent walking and some storm clouds rolled in. They all just pulled their hoods up and kept going without a word as it began to downpour. The Mimson Mountains loomed overhead, frowning down at them with pointy, dark gray disapproval.

Night came, and they had to find a decent place to sleep out of the weather. They split up and searched, and Dorky ended up finding a hole in the side of the mountain with a flat rock jutting out just above, like a little porch roof about eight feet high. There was enough room underneath for all of them to fit. Forky inspected it and noticed there was an old wooden door in the back of the little hole.

"What's that door? Did you check it out, Dorky?" he asked.

"Yeah, it probably isn't actually there," said Dorky; Forky nodded in agreement.

Everyone got out their sleeping bags and laid them out. Soon after, they were all asleep.

In the middle of the night, Bobill awoke to the sound of thunder. But it wasn't *all* thunder he was hearing. The ground started to shake and Bobill began to get frightened. Suddenly, he saw a flash, the ground rumbled once again. While Bobill was peeking through his eyes, he saw a huge boulder come out of the sky and land right in front of the hole. He jumped around it and ran out into the open pouring rain to hide, which was a very dumb idea.

Then he saw it: a Giant came out of nowhere, picked up the boulder, and attempted to throw it at another Giant off in the distance. The boulder seemed to take more of an upward trajectory than the first Giant may have thought.

Bobill watched as he just stood there for a moment looking into the distance, waiting in vain to see the massive stone hit the other Giant.

'SLAM!!!' The boulder landed on top of him and crushed him flat.

"I guess he didn't throw it far enough," Bobill thought to himself.

Realizing he was in the middle of a war with beings too big for his liking, he ran back into the little cave and discovered the Dorks were gone and that old door was sitting open. Seeing no other option, he high-tailed it down the tunnel after them. It didn't take long for Bobill to get lost. He found himself crawling at times and stumbling while tripping at others. While crawling, Bobill went through a little hole in the side of the cave wall. He fell through the dark, slamming walls back and forth over and over for what seemed like forever.

Finally, he hit a slope and slid to a stop in the mud. He stayed there for a few minutes, then slowly got up on all fours and began to crawl again. Just then he found something, it was quite circular, and he could fit his finger through it. He slipped it in his pocket and continued forward, thinking he would never get out of this cave.

Not long after that, he heard someone crying, "My Gracious! The Gracious is lost!!!"

Chapter 5:
Riddles with a Stinky Creature

Bobill soon came to a tunnel where he crawled toward the sound of the thing that was whining and whimpering.

He finally came near enough and hesitantly asked, "What's wrong?"

"What... is WRONG!?" said the whining creature in a raspy, crackly, fingernails-on-a-chalkboard voice. "US HAS LOST THE GRACIOUS!!! Does *it* know where it is?"

Bobill was a little confused at the moment from all the head slamming, but soon regained himself.

"No," he replied while straining his eyes in the dark to tell what exactly this weirdo even looked like.

Now, the creature was curious about Bobill, and it wondered if he had taken whatever this 'Gracious' was.

"Let's we play a game of riddles," said the creature.

Bobill, being frightened, nodded very quickly.

"If it loses, us will eat it. If it wins, it may eat we," said the creature.

Bobill shivered and replied, "How about you just show *me* how to get out of this place? It's slimy and cold and smells like buttocks down here."

The creature's eyes flashed with fiery irritation. "If *out* is what it wants... it will have more *respect* when in us's home," it said, in a mildly threatening tone.

Bobill nodded and gulped, then shakily insisted to the creature that *he* go first.

"Why did the chicken cross the road?" Bobill asked.

"*That* is not a RIDDLE! Must we eat it early, my Gracious?"

"NO PLEASE!!! I know I can think of something!"

So Bobill sat and thought for a while, then finally, he came up with one. "What has green hair, rolling locks, but no socks?" The creature just sat there for a moment with a dead, emotionless stare.

"*Seaweed*... it is," said the creature.

"Right..." replied Bobill, disappointed.

The creature was quite anxious for its turn.

"Now it is we's turn, my Gracious." The creature licked its lips several times in thought, then spoke. "As soon as it appears, then it's gone, the sight of it cuts through your eyes like the dawn, when it leaves, one dares to follow, like the deep crashing of drums in the hollow... what they be is?"

Bobill's mind wandered, and his eyes crossed for a moment. Suddenly, he snapped out of it and the answer came to him.

"That's easy," said Bobill. "Lightning and thunder... respectively."

The creature raspily sighed. "Now it's *its* turn... again."

Bobill again crossed his eyes while he thought, then said, "Here's a classic! Colors here and colors there, when the sun moves, there's not a moment to spare. The mist will fall, and night will call, if you don't look now, you might not see the colors at all. What am I?"

"Oh, us knowses this one," growled the creature. "It be a rainbow."

"Correct..." said Bobill who was getting very uneasy.

The creature scratched its head and thought a moment. "This is the one we's fat old gran made up years ago," it said. "They are the creatures of the night, searching for blood while in flight, they catch their prey then disappear, but this creature you should not fear, a closer look and you will find, that this creature is completely blind."

The creature barely finished and Bobill didn't even take time to make sure it was right; he already knew.

"This is so easy!" he said. "It's a flippin' bat! And I don't think they're actually blind so that was kind of a dumb one."

The creature looked at him with hate in its eyes. "It is the tasty little buttercake's turn again.... We mean man. The little *man's* turn."

Bobill was sick with fear, but he'd already thought up his next riddle at least. It came to him while answering the creature's last one.

"I have many arms but no eyes, these arms reaching to the skies. Deep in the earth, I do also lie."

The creature sat there a minute with a troubled look on its face. "Uhhhh... grrrrr... uhmmm... it's a tree!"

Bobill shifted in his uneasiness and gave a nod.

"Us's turn again, my Gracious..." said the creature. "Green—"

The creature was cut off by Bobill who screamed, "Grass!"

Now the creature was furious. With gritted teeth, it

replied, "Correct, my Gracious."

Bobill was very nervous by this time. He had no idea what to say to the creature. At least now he was more wary of its movements since his eyes had adjusted about as well as they ever would to the deep darkness of the cave. He could somewhat see the nasty thing crouched down only several feet away; its dead pale eyes fixed on him while squeezing what seemed to be a log or rock that looked a lot like Bobill's chubby neck. Bobill felt like he was going to lose it and start panicking, but he held it together until something finally came to him... one last riddle.

He cleared his throat and began melodically, "He is a thing that smells of decay, ask the way out and he will say, 'Gracious, oh Gracious! Where art thee? We're lost in the dark and us can't see!' He is, above all, the dumbest of creatures, with teeth like a monkey and fat facial features. He's ugly, stupid, and lives in a cave, do what he says, or you'll be his slave! His odor is foul, he's three feet tall, he is the smelliest creature of all!!"

The creature sat and thought for the longest time.

Bobill believed it had gone to sleep until he heard it mumbling to itself, "Smells of decay... dumbest of all creatures... fat facial features. Wait!! It's us!!! IT IS US!!!!"

The creature looked like it wanted to tear Bobill's head

off. It inched closer to Bobill with its eyes burning red and its teeth sticking out.

Suddenly it went right back to its normal-looking self and said, "It's us's turn, yet again.... Hmmm... let we think for a moment. Us gots one! Cold and clammy, nice and dandy, slippery slop—"

Bobill stopped him in his tracks again and blurted out, "EEL!"

"AHHHH! My Gracious!!! Must you always get them right!?"

Bobill crossed his eyes for a brief moment and went into deep thought.

"Aha! Bet you don't know this... *stinky*." Bobill whispered the last part as not to get himself on a dinner plate just yet. He'd gained a bit of confidence with the little scheme he had just cooked up. He folded his arms, leaned in slightly, and muttered: "Shiny and round, to the finger it's bound—what to do I have in me gym socks?"

The creature widened its eyes really hard and let out a shriek. "That is NOT fair! To ask we what it has in its *NASTY* little socketses!!"

Bobill looked at the creature for a moment, then said, "I suppose if you don't know, then you'll just have to show me the way out."

The creature quickly began trying to guess. "Ummmm... cheese or bread, maybe some lead. Maybe some fleas or maybe a sled. Could be a ball, could be a fox. Maybe some bells, or maybe some clocks. Box of locks? MORE gym socks? It could be rain—it could be snow. It probably isn't 'cuz WE DO NOT KNOW!!!"

Bobill was happy to know that he had won the riddle contest.

"Time to show me the way out of here, fellow," he said.

But the creature had other plans. Like such plans that of snacking on Bobill. The creature came closer and closer until Bobill accidentally slipped the ring on. To his surprise, it made him unseeable! When he realized the creature couldn't find him anywhere, Bobill ran away and looked for the exit. It wasn't that far away from where he was sitting, and it had an illuminated emergency exit sign above it. He should've just looked for it before. Nevertheless, he cooked beans getting out of that stinkhole. Though the brave Gabbin was out of the worst part of the caverns, he definitely wasn't out of the closely second worst part. Porks, infinillions of them.

It was their disgusting Pork kingdom he had just run into. He was invisible, but he was afraid of the beastly things smelling his little toots as he ran through the tunnels. He got very gassy when he was afraid. Several rights and half a dozen lefts later, he came to an archway that had many Porks standing in it. He waited for a moment, hoping they would leave, but they were just shootin' the breeze and gossiping like old ladies.

Suddenly... 'POOT!' All of the Porks looked at the spot where the sound had come from.

One of the largest of them shouted, "We've got a tiny invisible pooter amongst us!"

They started swinging axes and other sharpened objects at the sound and smell. Bobill ran as hard as he could and jumped about six inches in the air. It didn't help at all, but he ran under the legs of the brutes and kept on going. He eventually saw daylight down the tunnel. He stopped only for a moment just to check if he was being followed. The huge Porks had died from Bobill's poison gas leak. He continued out of a door that was ajar, and he saw no more Porks that day.

Bobill ran out into the sunlight which almost blinded him, since he'd been in total darkness for what seemed like ages. He searched for the Dorks for a few hours, and when he finally found them, they were sitting around a tree singing as usual.

Riddles with a Stinky Creature

"Around the tree, we sing this song!
We are free cuz Gabbin's gone!
He got lost and went astray,
now soon we'll be on our way!
Dootle-Doot-Doot!
Dootle-Doot-Doot...
Gabbin's gone, Gabbin's gone!
Gabbin's GONE!!!"

They shut their lips as soon as they saw Bobill.

"Let us move on," said Forky.

Bobill put up a hand. "Just a second now! How did you Dorks get out of that horrid cave?"

Jerky squawked up and said very quickly, "We cried like babies and told the Porks that we would make them a diamond castle if we could leave. They wanted one of us to stay and of course, we chose you. We went back to get you, but you were gone. So, we just ran away screaming and somehow made it."

Forky slapped the back of Jerky's head and said, "No, we... umm... KILLED ALL THE PORKS! Yes. Then we just walked on out of there, Gabbin. Right on out. Anyway, we should get moving."

They found the trail again and began to move along at a good pace. As a matter of fact, it seemed to Bobill that the pace quickened every ten steps he took. He soon realized that the Dorks were trying to outrun him so they wouldn't have to deal with him anymore. Bobill became enraged and started running as fast as he could. He first passed Corky, then came Slerky. Another fifteen running steps took Bobill past Porky and Jerky. Dorky and Forky were the only two left. Bobill looked at them with determination and started running harder than he had ever run before. Within thirty strides, he passed both Dorky and Forky. Bobill became proud and started running even faster. Suddenly, he heard... nothing. He looked back and the Dorks were gone. Bobill slid to a stop and looked around. Nothing.

He sat on the ground and grumbled, "Where is Randolf...."

Just about that time, Bobill heard a roaring noise louder than the time all of the pots fell out of his kitchen cabinets. The Dorks came flying by with smoke and fire behind them. Bobill looked up and saw a bronze figure fly out of the woods and right into Forky Rottenfield. Next came Dorky, then Slerky, then Jerky, then Porky, and last came Corky. They had all slammed into each other like a cheese sandwich on a cold sunny day.

Randolf popped his head out from all the Dorks and said valiantly, "Let's get going! We are to visit my good friend Neebo in the morning. He doesn't know me, but we are friends don't you worry!"

The company trudged on through the night without much conversation. Actually, Randolf didn't really give a hoot about what they had just been through. All the time they were frightened by every little noise and movement around them.

Chapter 6:
Neebo

At last, they came to Neebo's lands in the early morning. Off in the distance, they could see his enormous house or cabin made of sticks. It was really more like a stick-mansion. They passed further in and came past fences with giraffes and penguins in them. At one point, Randolf had to hit Porky over the head with his staff when he tried to yank one of the penguins out from behind the fence and cook it, swearing on his pants that it was a chicken in a wedding suit. The company came up to the front porch of the mansion; around it, there were all kinds of flowers and herbs growing everywhere. This guy seemed like a nature man. Randolf smacked the door with his staff, and they waited as loud footsteps echoed through the mansion.

'Click, click, clickety. Crack, crizzle, creeeeaaaakkk!' The gigantic door slowly opened, and the company beheld Neebo. A nine-foot-tall man that looked a lot like a gorilla.

He was fully covered in thick, dark fur aside from his

face and wearing absolutely nothing but a pair of dark blue jeans. Bobill was creeped out to no end as the gorilla man's big eyes beamed at them all. Randolf bowed in respect and began to talk but was cut off....

"Who the heck are you!?" yelled Neebo.

Randolf replied, "Let me explain, good sir. I am Randolf—you may have heard of me. I am a great and powerful *Wizard*!!"

He waved his hands high in the air and Neebo just glared at him.

"I have heard of a Randolf. Heard he was a fool."

Randolf chuckled. "Not *that* Randolf. I am Randolf... the *non*-fool."

Neebo's eyebrows raised slightly. "Well then, any non-fool is welcome in my household. Come in, I was about to have some breakfast. Golden buttercakes and imitation bacon."

They all went inside and were served breakfast at a large table exactly like the ones gorillas prefer. There was also a fireplace bigger than Bobill's entire home at the end of the dining hall. BellJohn himself would have swooned at the sight of it.

As they ate, Randolf explained to Neebo about all that

had transpired with the Porks in the mountain caves, while Bobill tried to figure out how Randolf even knew.

"Filthy things, those Porks," said Neebo. "Hate them with a passion. See that over there?" He pointed to a huge red stick in the corner, it was covered in spikes and such. "That sucker didn't use to be red if ya know what I'm saying. Cracked many a Pork over the dome with ol' Sue. Then I painted her red."

Randolf nodded, trying with all his might to look like he cared about anything Neebo was saying. He really only cared to brag about his own adventures, but not to say too much... he liked to be mysterious. He also liked to brag about how mysterious he was.

Eventually, Neebo got up and told them he had some gardening to do. "You can take a look at my library if you wish. There are many books in that room."

The guests entered the library and Bobill found some books to his liking. Such as gardening books and cheese books and books about being scared of going outside. The Dorks just read books about gold and Dragons. Possibly a title on how to go about keeping one's pickaxe rust-free or how to properly walk without stepping on one's own beard. Neebo had amassed quite the collection over the years.

While they read, Neebo sat in a large cushiony chair on

the other side of the room and quietly played his antique accordion.

"I thought he said he had some *gardening* to attend to," said Jerky in a classically obnoxious tone while using his hand like a mouth to say the word 'gardening'.

Neebo shot a glance at the rude Dork, his hearing being better than Jerky had anticipated.

"It's apparent the Dork knows nothing of how to tend a garden," said Neebo, who kicked a book across the floor to Jerky.

The title was, 'How to Grow Fabulous Plants Using a Musical Squeeze-Box'. Jerky was shocked. He flipped the book open to find that every page was blank. Puzzled, he looked back up at Neebo. He was gone, the chair empty and accordion hanging neatly on the wall. His now totally confused eyes lowered down once more to the book. It had vanished as well, and only his flat palms were seen.

"Bobill," said Jerky shakily, "where did Neebo and the book go?" His eyes were fearful and wide, darting around the room.

Bobill turned around and casually answered, "Who's Neebo?"

Jerky jumped to his feet, throwing his arms around

himself in a nearing panic.

Just before he let out a scream of terror, Bobill chuckled and added, "Calm down, Jerky. Neebo thought you were being kind of, well... jerky. So, he hypnotized you with his ape-gaze, then spent half an hour explaining to the rest of us how he was teaching you a lesson by freaking out your mind with a fake blank book that didn't exist. Then he cleaned his accordion, hung it up on the wall, and rushed to the door mumbling about how he had forgotten to tend to his plants. We heard him snap his fingers loudly just as he went out, then you suddenly came to your senses and asked where he and the non-existent book had gone."

Jerky stared at Bobill a moment, then laughed slightly. "Oh yeah, I know, I was playing along. Can't fool this brain with no hypno-tricks. Joke's on him!" he said, laughing again. He then got up, moved to a corner by himself, and read a book about how to read books.

The group spent several hours in the library until they became extremely bored, so Corky brought up an idea for a plan for the lot of them to look around outside the stuffy, lame place. Randolf was busy shining his tarnished bronze slippers and waved them away, annoyed with their whining. The Dorks and Bobill all walked out the back door into the well-tended backyard.

Out behind Neebo's house, they found astonishing

sights. The landscaping skills that had been utilized in that area were unprecedented to say the very least. They (mostly Bobill) gazed in amazement as they slowly walked farther back into the property. Little stony streams ran here and there, a path crossing each of them with well-crafted, wooden bridges. An immense pond welcomed them halfway across the yard, containing all manner of fish and waterbirds. Bobill took this chance to show the Dorks his proficiency at rock skipping. They waited impatiently as Bobill's rocks plopped straight in without a hint of skippage.

"I can do it! I promise you! I'm just a little rusty is all," said he.

Then he found it, the perfect skipping stone. It was wide, flat, and had some weight to it. It fit his chubby little hand better than he could've imagined. He hated to even throw it. But this was his big moment. With a look of dead-serious determination, he took a deep breath, slid back one foot, and started winding up. He was going to put some pepper on this baby. The Gabbin stepped forth in a flash, cast his arm to full outstretch, and released the stone. It momentarily tore through the open air, quickly striking the water's glassy surface at a flawless twenty-degree angle and skipped; not once, not thrice, but sixty-four times it leapt off the top of the liquidy pool. Bobill grinned so hard that he injured his face, but it was well worth it. He turned to see the Dorks' expressions, but every one of them was asleep, heaped in a pile upon an iron bench.

Even worse, the last skip sent the rock straight into an angry egret who had just settled down for lunch. The bird came at Bobill over the water at blinding speed and attempted to skewer his eyeballs. Bobill wailed like a little baby-man and sprinted off, shouting at the Dorks as he ran by them. The Dorks jumped up from their sleep and were met with relentless egret attacks as Bobill sped away. Soon, they too had run, then caught up with Bobill.

After many minutes of pursuit, the bird eventually turned back to its pond. With hearts pounding and lungs wheezing, the group finally stopped and found themselves at a large, reinforced iron gate that looked like it was supposed to be somewhat hidden. After catching his breath, Forky examined it very thoroughly and came to the conclusion that he wanted to see what was on the other side. Just when he began to pull out his pry bar, Neebo showed up.

"What's going on back here, fellows?" he asked with an eyebrow raised.

"Nothin'," replied Forky as fast as possible, sounding quite nervous and dropping his arms to his sides.

Neebo cracked a grin and switched the raised eyebrow to the other side. Jerky shuffled back a few paces, looking away.

"You small folk want to know what I keep in there?" asked Neebo.

Bobill yelled, "YES PLEASE! I mean... sure, whatevs."

Neebo told them he needed to get the key, so he returned to the house to retrieve it. Within minutes he was speedwalking back to them again. He winked at them with both eyes at the same time and produced a three-foot key from his massive pocket.

"There are many wondrous and magical things on the other side of this gate... prepare yourselves."

He jammed the key into a keyhole that was quite inconspicuous. It turned with a loud creak, then they all heard a 'Ka-Click!' Neebo lifted his large foot high in the air and kicked the gate open.

He turned toward the group with a frightful grin and said, "Right this way, fellows!"

He led them down a long path that eventually came to an enormous field.

Forky was getting uneasy about the whole affair and questioned Neebo. "What exactly is this place, sir?"

Neebo was more serious now. "This is my greatest

accomplishment. I have brought back creatures which were once extincted!"

The group stared at him in amazement but had no idea what he was talking about.

Dorky broke the silence and whined, "What kind of creatures? Like... *bugs*?"

"Heck no," said Neebo. "More like... lizards... GREAT big friggin' lizards."

The Dorks and Bobill could not have gotten their eyes much wider. For in the distance, they saw a Practosaurus, which had died out over five thousand years before. It was one of the largest creatures to ever exist and had a neck that was nearly three hundred feet long. The rest of its body, including the tail, was another whole seventy-five feet long. It was eating out of a tall tree in the middle of the field.

Neebo smiled at their reaction and said, "Welcome... to Dinoriffic Park."

When the group had recovered from fainting, Forky asked Neebo, "How is this possible?"

Neebo answered him. "I will show thee."

Chapter 7:
A Stroll in the Park

After a bit more walking, the group came to a building. Neebo led them inside and explained how he came upon this miracle.

"One day, I was experimenting on feeding my lizards rocks instead of insects, because rocks are very easy to find. What I didn't know, is that they were not just plain old rocks. I had fed a male lizard a ground-up dinosaur bone fossil, and to a female, I fed some ground-up uranium. The female laid some eggs months later... and now, I have a whole bunch of dinosaurs!"

Corky asked, "What about the ones that eat meats? I read about those kinds in books."

"The animals are in large metal cages that I built myself. They cannot escape."

So, they all decided to go back out to see the safe and fun meat-eaters.

The group hiked across the secret fenced-in valley behind Neebo's house and down a winding path through thick, ancient forest, coming at last to a clearing that contained the enormous cages of the meat-eaters. There were a few in rows on each side of the area. All of them were wide open and empty.

"Well, *that* isn't good," said Neebo. "I could've SWORN I locked those.... Oh well, we should probably get going. I have some delicious bass cooking back at the cottage. Wouldn't want to be late for supper, eh?"

The huge man quickly spun on his heel and began briskly walking back up the woodland path, trying to look as calm as possible.

Slerky then whispered, voice cracking, "Let's get going. I'm pretty sure things are NOT okay!"

They were not at all. In fact, the group was only now beginning to notice the droplets of rain falling through the leaves overhead, the darkening skies, and the low distant rumble of thunder. Neebo was already out of sight and the group took off running in the direction he'd gone. The only problem was, they had actually gone the exact opposite way by mistake. It was getting darker by the second and the rain fell heavier.

Still running and starting to panic, they all kept

bumping into trees and each other. They swished through soaking wet bushes and tangling vines, getting more and more hopelessly lost in the ominous forest. All the while knowing they could be attacked by nightmare creatures not seen since ages past at any moment. Then it happened. Forky, out ahead sprinting with all his might down a weed-infested slope, slammed face-first into a very large, leathery, crooked... thing. He felt it with his hand and began backing away as it moved a little. He squinted in the fading light and could see now that it was one of the big plant-eating animals.

He sighed in relief just before a terrible head peeked up over it. The plant-eater was lying on its side, dead as anything, and one of the loose meat-eaters was going to town on the other side. Forky stayed motionless, thinking that perhaps the beast hadn't noticed him yet. He'd creep away silently and go back the way he came....

'SLAMM!!' Porky had run full speed into Forky, followed by the rest of the Dorks. They all smashed into the carcass hard.

Bobill managed to slide to a stop in the mud and weeds a few feet short of the Dork-pile. Suddenly, a huge, clawed foot stomped down on the side of its disturbed kill. It raised itself up, looking down over the cowering, pathetic group of soaked Dorks. Bobill crawled behind a nearby tree, hoping he was out of sight. The meat-eater was large, maybe twenty feet in length.

It stared unblinking at the Dorks for a moment. Dorky had seen a drawing of this creature long ago in Dork-school. What was its name? Yes, it came to him. It was without a doubt the Turklufortchlidon. At least the second or third fiercest dinosaur that ever lived. Steam rolled from the flared nostrils of its long snout. Gray with black stripes it was, with piercing yellow eyes that seemed to glow in the darkness.

It bared its endless rows of fangs lining its powerful jaws, then let out a mighty shrieking scream.

'EEEaaaaRRRKKK!!'

The Dorks sprung to action, jumping right to their feet, all slamming face-first into each other and falling flat on their backs. Then they jumped back up again to speed off into the night. Bobill peeked around his tree in time to see the dino give chase and disappear. He had no idea what to do; nonetheless, he decided to just run after them. As he ran, he tripped on a tree root and landed hard, flipping over several times. The poor fellow rubbed his sore head, and as he did, he heard a sound coming from a large tree nearby.

"Psst!!" someone said. It was Forky.

The rest of the Dorks were huddled behind him in the

hollow of the tree.

"Over there!" He pointed at an old rusty minecart sitting on some tracks.

Bobill nodded as they all regrouped and stepped lightly over to it. They piled in, but before Bobill had gotten his leg over, Jerky had released the brake. All of the Dorks whizzed away in the cart and Bobill began sprinting with all his might.

Corky leaned over the back. "Run, Master Gabbin! Run!" he cried, reaching out his hand desperately.

Bobill somehow caught up.

He threw forth his arm trying to grab the outstretched hand, and Corky yanked it back a few times, saying, "Too slow! Too slow!!"

An enraged Bobill then leapt forward, biting down hard into the Dork's little hand. "aaaaAAAHHH!!" screamed Corky, as he started slapping Bobill's face with his other hand.

But little Bobill wouldn't loosen his mouthy grip. His small, frail body flapping wildly in the wind behind the ever-increasing speed of the minecart. Out of nowhere, the Turklufortchlidon appeared from the weeds of their left side, narrowly missing Bobill's toes with its razor-sharp fangs. The creature's pace quickened after its missed opportunity while the minecart headed downhill and into some swerving turns. Branches were overhead and the Dorks often had to duck to keep from being beaned in the face by them. The dino however, snapped through them like buttersticks; it was catching up. Bobill wished he could scream; Corky wished he could stop screaming. Jerky was trying his best to steer the cart without anything whatsoever to steer with and Forky, Dorky, Porky, and Slerky were throwing small rocks they found in the cart at the dinosaur, mostly hitting Bobill.

The dinosaur was now within reach. It outstretched its long neck, mouth open preparing to take off Bobill's lower half. Just as the jaws began to close, something incredible happened. A massive shape barreled in from their right, taking the Turklufortchlidon's side into its very much larger mouth and slamming it down to the ground. The group sped away from the awful sounds that came from the attack and Corky finally pulled Bobill in. A minute or so later, they squinted in the dark ahead to see that the tracks ended directly into a large boulder. Not a moment too soon, they all dove for their lives as the minecart flattened like a flatcake into the side of the unforgiving stone. Aching all over and soaked to the bone, they all attempted to sit up and assess the situation.

Slerky then cried out, "Look there!" as an absolutely

monumental behemoth of a dinosaur slowly walked forth from the blackness they had come from. It was swallowing the last bit of the Turklufortchlidon's tail and eyeing them hungrily.

"That... is the undisputed king of the dinosaurs," said Dorky. "Or so I've heard.... It is called Gerrogarguthosaurus: The Unkindest of Super Lizards."

Forky sighed. "We have no choice," he said, unsheathing his sword. "We are cornered and cannot outrun it. We must slay this wretched beast."

The rest drew their weapons as well, not looking nearly as confident as Forky. The insanely large monster dino stepped toward them. Blood red, slashed with wild, sharp, ashen striping down its sixty-foot back, it glared at the group with fire in its black-slitted, wicked, red eyes. It lowered its nose down, displaying the long, jagged, curved horn that tipped it, then threw its head skyward, roaring like nothing they had ever heard.

'OOOAAARRRRR!!!' it boomed, shaking them to the core.

The Dorks dropped their weapons and covered their ears. Death was upon them. The mighty creature charged; like an earthquake it was.

Bobill, without thinking, slipped on his ring and bolted

away in fear. *"They always leave me! What's the harm in ME doing it for once?"* he thought.

The Dorks gathered themselves and reached for their weapons yet again. They screamed with swords and axes raised, the dinosaur roared again as it closed in only a few dozen yards away. Fifty feet, forty, thirty, twenty... it lowered its huge head and opened wide, about to imminently swallow them all whole.

'CRASH!!'

Something just as big as the Gerrogarguthosaurus slammed into it. A black mountain of fur it seemed. Bobill stopped and looked back at the commotion. It was Neebo. He had somehow transformed into a Super Ape and was smashing the living crap out of the giant lizard. But it fought back, snapping at his face, then breaking loose from his grip to swing its tail around and sweep his legs out from under him. The dino was on top of him now, ready to go for the throat.

Neebo rolled backward and jumped to his feet. He gathered all his strength, looked over at the Dorks and Bobill (who had removed the ring and rejoined the group), gave them a cleverly knowing, yet apologetically un-sorry and heroically valiant wink with both eyes simultaneously.

Then, he brought down his iron ape-fist square into the

dino's face with a violent, raging 'BOOOM!!!'

There was a large crater where the dinosaur once stood when the smoke cleared. Bobill and the Dorks simply fainted and remembered no more until the next morning.

Bobill awoke to the smell of honey and buttercakes. He rubbed his eyes and saw all of the Dorks sprawled out sleeping and snoring in various positions around Neebo's living room. In the corner, Randolf was polishing the last square inch of his left bronze slipper.

"That'll about do it," said Randolf, admiring his reflection in the sides of the gleaming footwear.

Bobill had a headache and an everything-else ache. His arms were scratched up, there were bandages in various places and the Dorks didn't look much better. As he was remembering what happened the night before, Neebo stepped into the room. He had a three-foot, cylindrical, white hat on his head, an apron upon his great forefront, mittens on both hands, and he held a wooden tray of many wondrous breakfast-time foods. He winked at Bobill with both eyes.

"Up already I see!" said the apelike man. "I prepared a large breakfast, and enough to pack and take with you on the rest of your journey."

As the Dorks sat up, rubbing their eyes, confused to

high heavens, and mumbling things like, 'That little tub of lard didn't even get eaten!', Bobill began to ask the burning question in his mind.

"Is everything okay? What happened with the dino—"

"That didn't happen," Neebo interrupted quickly, setting the tray down on the living room table.

Bobill was concerned, but set to eating anyhow, as did the Dorks and Randolf.

After they had finished, Randolf told Neebo, "We are so thankful for your hospitality, friend. I believe after we have rested only two more days here, we shall be ready to brave the deadly darkness that awaits us ahead."

Neebo said nothing in reply but walked outside, lifted up one end of the house, and waited for the Bobill, Randolf, and the Dorks to slide out on to the ground.

"Leaving so soon?" asked Neebo, casually walking around the side of his cabin. "Shame... it was good to have company."

"Well..." began Randolf.

Neebo cut him right off. "I packed you some butter sandwiches and cheese waffles for the road. You can use my camel, Braunsvag, to reach the forest, though you must send him back upon arriving there—camels are no place for woods."

Randolf crossed his eyes and said, "Ohh, yes, yes, we should be going. Thank-you muchly, my good Neebo, it has been a pleasure."

Neebo gave a slight look of grim wariness and added, "Beware that place yonder, travelers. Therein dwells distant kinsman of mine who have become strange and possibly even belligerent and incorrigible in their dark solitude. Trust none of them."

The group absolutely wasn't listening whatsoever. They grabbed their bags and started off, each one saying a quick thanks to Neebo. Bobill was last and couldn't help but gaze to the gate in the distance where he was sure they had actually entered the previous night. The gate was sitting open.

Bobill then said, "Many thanks to you, sir. You have been most kind, and your secret gate is quite open."

Neebo's eyes grew wide. "SHOOT!" he exclaimed, looking first down at his pants, but then turning and running towards the gate.

"Goodbye then," said Bobill.

They all climbed atop the extraordinarily large camel that was lent to them and were off.

Chapter 8:
Kirkwoods

After they had taken Braunsvag as far as they were able to on a rather long, boring, and uneventful trip (aside from the one really crazy incredible part that I won't mention), the group arrived at the next stage. And what a harsh stage it would be... for they had to travel through... Kirkwoods. One of the most dangerous and creepy wooded areas in Skiddle Earth.

They unloaded their belongings, slinging their heavy packs over their shoulders. Randolf then slapped Braunsvag on his camquarters, and he bolted like a torpedo into the distance, back to the safety of the house of Neebo. Then he, the Dorks, and Bobill stood in front of the entrance for a while, wondering if they should go in or just go around. If they went around, it would be three hundred fifty-seven miles out of the way, as Randolf knew well. After two days of thinking and eating most of their supplies, they decided to enter the woods of Kirkwoods.

All except Randolf that is.

"I have some things to check up on," he said. "You will have to make it without me a while."

Of course, the Dorks complained and told him he always took off when they really needed him, but Bobill was most afraid. Traveling the unknown, ancient, evil forest with only the rude Dorks sounded like an awful time indeed.

"Oh, get over it, you fat whine-bags!" yelled Randolf. "I believe I have helped more than enough already. But I assure you, once I'm done making sure I didn't leave my stove on... I mean, make sure... that I do some really courageous and important things, I will try and catch up with you when I can."

So away he went, leaving the very sad and pathetic rest of the group to figure out what to do on their own.

"Good riddance, you dumb, bearded geezer," Jerky said, just before a possibly random rock hit him between the eyes, knocking him to the ground.

The rest helped him up, sighed a long miserable sigh, and turned to the woods. There was nothing to do but proceed now.

About twenty or thirty steps into the woods, a very

large duck came up to Bobill and said, "Answer this riddle and you shall pass!"

The duck started to tell Bobill the riddle, but Bobill stuck his dagger in the duck's eyeball then poured salt in it. The duck stepped aside and let them in. The Gabbin was in quite the mood, and he'd certainly had enough of riddles for one story. The company was on their way again, and the smell of foul cheese was in the air. Bobill had known, but could now really sense it: this wasn't going to be a pleasant walk through these woods. They had about five hundred miles to walk, and it was so dark they couldn't even see their toes in front of their faces. Who knows how long it would take?

There was a small path winding through the darkness that they knew they mustn't leave... lest they be lost in the maddening blackness for all time. After a good long while, maybe hours or a couple of days, they seemed to be able to see somewhat. Whether it simply took a long time to get used to, or they were just lying to themselves, they were not sure. Here and there they would, on occasion, see eerie sights. Such as black ducks frowning at them from around a tree, only to quickly run away. Bobill thought one of them had a knife maybe. Little fuzzy bug-eyed rat monkeys also there were, or might've been, scurrying across the path and making strange clicky, chittery noises.

Once, Porky swore he saw a little man in a pointy hat with a dim lantern beckoning them to come have a dinner of cheesecorn and beans. Forky told him to ignore it, and for all of them to ignore the sights and sounds, and just move forward.

"A magical place this is," said he. "It is known to goof around with one's mind and lure one deep into the unknown reaches, swallowed by the forest itself for sustenance."

Bobill shuddered at the thought. On they went, and around a quarter of the way through, they saw a glow in the distance. They crept up slowly and quietly to get a look at what it could be. There, just off the side of the path in a small clearing, someone, or something sat. It was an elderly monkey. He waved at them immediately and pointed to a nametag on his hairy chest that claimed his name was 'Gorizzle the Fiddler'. He had a fire going with roast buttons over it. He said nothing, but motioned for them to come and partake.

The group couldn't believe their eyes, they were sure it was a hallucination. But there he stood, offering very real-looking food, which they had a difficult time of turning down considering they had eaten nearly all of their supplies. As they ate, Gorizzle played his fiddle and danced for hours. At one point, Bobill noticed the Dorks whispering amongst themselves about him. He made out a few words like 'fatty' and 'Mr. stupid man'. He rolled his eyeballs and pretended not to hear.

Eventually, everyone went to sleep listening to Gorizzle's fiddle softly playing. Early in the morning, or whatever time it was, Bobill woke to find Gorizzle had eaten Dorky and was chasing Slerky around a tree. Bobill grabbed his dagger and started waving it at the monkey's face. Gorizzle didn't care, he kept chasing Slerky. Finally, Bobill challenged him to a fiddling contest. They worked out the rules to be that if Bobill won, they could leave. If he lost, Gorizzle would eat them all.

The old monkey grabbed his bow and played his fiddle hard. He danced back and forth with his eyes closed until he started sweating and his legs buckled, Gorizzle fell to his knees breathing heavily while Bobill finished making a fiddle out of twigs and other junk.

Bobill looked hard Gorizzle. "You're good, but now... feel my wrath!"

He stuck his bow straight up in the air for a second or two, then whipped it down against the strings. The sound that followed was the greatest thing any of them had ever heard. Without shaking or breaking a sweat, he completed his awesome display of fiddlery. Bobill stood there silent for a moment... then he slammed the fiddle on Gorizzle's head.

The monkey fell on his face and the company again moved on through the woods. As they went, Bobill grew more uneasy. He didn't wish to be stuck alone with the Dorks who wanted to leave him back in the tunnels with that riddling creature and nearly let him get eaten by dinosaurs. Even if he *was* down by one Dork now, which the rest of them didn't seem to really notice.

If not for him, they would've all been consumed by that freakish primate back there. What other wretched things lay ahead? Would he have to get them out of every pickle they got into? Bobill shook his head, knowing that if he didn't brace himself, take a deep breath and continue, that any kind of book that could be written about him in the future would seem quite unfinished.

The group still couldn't see almost anything. It was most likely night and darn near pitch black. Bobill was following Slerky when suddenly he heard Corky trip over Forky, who had stopped to admire the view. Jerky and Porky freaked out because they thought that Gorizzle the Fiddler had come back to eat them all. Bobill tried calming them, but it was no use. They were screaming and running in circles with their hands in the air.

They began punching, then swinging swords and axes at each other and Bobill while yelling, "AHHHH MONKEYS! MONKEYS I TELL YOU!!!"

THE GABBIN

Bobill flung himself out of the way just in time, and somehow none of them managed to seriously injure each other. They finally stopped and fell to their behinds. The hunger and darkness were getting to them. Everyone then moved on. No one knew what time of day it was, so they walked until their eyes started shutting. Forky was the first one to collapse, and then came the rest on top of him. Bobill laid himself down next to the tower of Dorks and fell asleep not long after his head hit the ground.

The next day, Bobill awoke to find Randolf sitting on the top of the pile of Dorks smoking his five-foot-long magic bubble pipe and drinking green coffee. Bobill was more than overjoyed to see him but didn't ask Randolf any questions about where he had been, for he knew that the wizard would just give an annoyed and mysterious remark about how it was none of his business. So Bobill and Randolf woke the Dorks up by whacking them with sticks, and they were off again on another dark day of traveling.

At about five hours into their traveling that day, they came across a black stream that crossed the path and sounded like it was drinkable. By the time Randolf had told the Dorks and Bobill that the stream was too dangerous to drink, Porky was already rolling around in it with his tongue hanging out the side of his face, slurping up the water. Randolf pulled Porky out of the water and laid him on the ground. At first, he didn't move or even blink.

All of the sudden, he grew very large and hair sprouted all over him. His chubby little Dork mouth turned into huge jaws and his ears grew pointy. Porky's eyes turned yellow, then red, then black, then red again.

Randolf looked at the company and said calmly, "RUN, YOU DARN DORKS! RUN!!!!"

They all took off, Bobill was running and hiding every few steps. The rest of the Dorks just kept running into each other and falling down like dummies. Pork the Beast came at them howling horribly. He had transformed into... a Were-Dork. Randolf jumped high and swung through the trees at hundreds of miles per hour until he was out of the woods, leaving the Dorks and Bobill with Pork the Beast. The other Dorks had an idea, they would drink the water and fight him, then everything would be fine. So, they started sipping the water and also became Were-Dorks. Fork, Pork, Cork, Slerk, and Jerk the Beasts came after Bobill immediately. He ran down the trail and about an hour later he had reached the three-quarters-of-the-way-through point. Out stepped an elderly Gorilla named Monkizzle the Guittler.

Monkizzle said, in a rather fancy and sophisticated tone of voice, "I will eat every bit of you if you can't beat me in an electric guitar contest."

So Bobill grabbed some rocks and vines and

begrudgingly began to construct an electric guitar. Bobill took quite a while to make this instrument, considering he had no idea what an electric guitar was. In fact, it took him an hour, but thankfully the Were-Dorks had still not arrived.

All the while, Monkizzle had built a fire for them to be able to see for judging form and style. Bobill finished his masterpiece just in time to see Monkizzle the Guittler plug his guitar into a rock, jump up into the air and start jamming. Bobill watched as Monkizzle the Guittler played his crazy jungle tunes on his green electric guitar while doing the moonwalk up a sequoia tree. He landed on a branch, took off his glasses and put them in the pocket of his denim vest. Then he pulled out his hairpin, loosing his flowing blonde locks down almost to his black skin-tight leather pants. He swung his hair in circles and kicked his pure white platform shoes against the tree as he shredded away.

When Monkizzle finished his solo, Bobill just stared, soaking it all in and trying to process what he'd just witnessed. He then planted his foot on a rock so he could rest his guitar-like contraption on his knee. Bobill began plucking at the bottom string, and it sounded horrible. He sat there for a moment with his eyes crossed.

"Now I remember!" he cried.

Bobill started his fret-blazing leads which quickly turned into a jamming tune. The intricate weave of metal rhythm and unreal harmonics filled the minds of all who heard with wonder and joy. He picked the strings flawlessly, and faster than a bolt of lightning with a 500 shot of nitrous. No song had ever been played like it, and none ever since. When he finished on a long screaming note, he pulled a 360 up on one toe, cracking Monkizzle in the teeth with his stone guitar. Monkizzle flipped around and crashed face-first into the forest floor. The Mighty Gorilla had finally been defeated.

Bobill then turned his attention to the angry Dorks storming down the path toward him. Even though he, nor they could see anything due to the darkness of the forest, Bobill was still quite concerned. He could hear it now... the Dorks were eating everything in their path as they rampaged the forest. It sounded like the Dorks were moving at a fairly rapid pace... something that he had now realized the Dorks were known for. He quickly thought of what to do, deciding to climb a tree until the Dorks passed him by.

As soon as he got situated in the tree and was comfortable, the tree came out from underneath him. Off went the Dorks as they ate every tree, bush, and speck of dirt that stood in their path. Bobill lay on the ground totally unconscious as they ran off. He woke up with a bright light in his eyes. It was the sun! This was something that he had not seen for many days. The Dorks had eaten so much that they allowed sunlight to penetrate into the dark woods.

"I must find Randolf," he muttered under his breath. "These Dorks have gone too far!"

Bobill then turned to the path ahead and started down it. He was glad to be able to see again. By evening he had spotted the exit of the forest. As he grew near to it, he realized how truly sick he was of being in this place, so he started running.

He thought to himself, *"Just a little further and I'll be out of—"*

Randolf jumped out of the trees right into Bobill's path. They both slammed into each other and went tumbling out of the forest.

"Thought you'd be out of here already," said Randolf.

"No, I had some business to attend to. *All* of the Dorks are turned to monsters now and beat me out of here," said Bobill.

"Let us go find the Dorks before they eat everything in sight!" said Randolf with a concerned voice.

"How did you know the Dorks were eating everything, Randolf?" asked Bobill.

Randolf pulled back his staff and struck Bobill in the cranium. When he awoke, they were behind a small bush in the middle of a huge field. Randolf was peeking over it watching the Dorks eat a herd of buffalos.

He looked down at Bobill. "Oh, I see that you are awake now," he said. "I'm going to go out there and hit them over the head with my Anti-Were-Dork Staff, which is what I left to go get before. I always leave it lying within several dozen miles of enchanted streams that Dorks may attempt to drink from. Prepare yourself, my good Bobill, this may get *nasty*."

Randolf jumped over the bush doing a triple flip. Bobill tried to look away from Randolf's flapping kilt but breathed a slight sigh of relief when he realized that underneath, Randolf was wearing blue short-shorts dotted with alternating pictures of bronze staffs and little pointy yellow hats. The Wizard ran toward the Dorks yelling like a crazy person.

Slerk the Beast spotted Randolf and charged him. His jaws opened to catch Randolf in them, but Randolf faked him out with a one-two slide step, spinning and curving all the way around him on one foot like a top. Slerk the Beast turned, and with another triple flip, Randolf bopped him on the head on the way over. Slerk the Beast transformed back into regular Dorkish Slerky again.

Randolf continued to Pork, Cork, and Jerk the Beasts. They rushed at him all at the same time in a closing cone of attack. Randolf, like a Quintuple Chromebelt Master of Kickchop, cartwheeled directly to his left, steering the trio of

Were-Dorks into a single file line. He quickly slid to a stop, digging his bronze slippers into the ground. Saving the triple flip this time, he instead ran right at them, and in a full-on sprint, he dove with all his might, sailing just over their heads.

'Bop-bop-bop!' All three were instantly changed back, looking like they had no idea what had just taken place.

Randolf now had but one Dork to change back... Fork the Beast, the meanest one. He stared at Randolf from a distance for a few moments, hunched down, clawing at the ground and snorting in a rage. Suddenly, he started toward Randolf. He was coming fast and was only thirty feet away now. Randolf stood his ground without movement. Ten feet. Five. Two and a half feet now! One!! THREE-SEVENTHS OF AN INCH!!! Randolf, like a bolt of greased cheese, jumped, did a single front flip, and double bopped Fork on the head so hard that his face literally made a sizeable crater in the dirt.

As he lay, tasting bitter earth, he changed back to normal old Forky Rottenfield again. Bobill, in total shock of Randolf's secret abilities, ran over to join them. Then they all awkwardly chuckled, nodded to each other, and went on; none of them ever speaking of that day again, and the Dorks never knowing what had truly happened.

Chapter 9:
Bread Ridges

Leaving the terrible woods behind, their next path would lead them through a place known as 'The Bridges of Bread Ridges'.

Bread Ridges was a very deep hole with hundreds of pieces of land sticking up like impossibly tall pillars throughout it. Each piece of land was connected by a junky old wood and rope bridge. As they approached, Slerky was telling Bobill of how his Great Uncle Clerky had led a team of Dorks to construct these bridges around nine hundred years ago. Bobill did not want to walk on the bridges at all and asked why they couldn't go around.

"Because it is a three hundred fifty-seven-mile journey around it!" exclaimed Randolf.

Bobill was just about to start protesting and maybe even mention that he could see all of the edges of the chasm and it wasn't nearly that far. But Randolf instantly leaned in at him with eyes growing large and menacing. His long, bronze eyebrows raised high, and he said this:

"Do not be deceived by those chubby little circles above your nose, Bobill, a Wizard's peep-spheres can measure any and all of the distances of the world."

Bobill, nervously looking around and sweating, gulped and said, "I mean uhh... let's go, Rando."

Randolf smiled, frowned, and nodded. Then, they started across the bridge to get to the first piece of land. Bobill dared to have a look down below a little past the halfway point, only to see mist and darkness.

Randolf said, "The holes here are so deep that none know exactly what is down there. It is about a five hundred mile fall as the rock flies, but maybe there are pillows at the bottom."

Bobill thought about what Randolf had said while he walked across the bridge that was swaying violently in the breeze. As soon as they all safely reached land, the bridge snapped apart and fell. They traveled across the small piece of land, reached the next bridge, and saw that it had fallen as well. All was gone save one worn out and frayed rope that was still strung across.

"I have crossed far more dangerous walkways than this," said Forky with the utmost sincerity.

The Dorks, one by one, all ran on their toes across to the other side. Bobill refused to go, so Randolf grabbed him by the back of his little pants and threw him over. He landed with great force, face first in the dirt at the Dorks' feet. Bobill got up and dusted himself off, then they all waited for Randolf to come with them. Randolf started walking on the rope, bronze slippers in one hand, staff in the other, but he didn't want them to know he had a hard time with balance. He tried to walk casually until he slipped off and caught himself with his left pinky toe.

He looked up at Bobill and the Dorks and said, "Go, you dummies!"

His toe slipped off the rope and he fell, bronze kilt and yellow beard flapping, into the blackness. The Dorks grabbed Bobill and ran over the next several bridges with him, each one exploding into dust the moment the last of them lifted their back foot off of it until they stopped to make camp on the center and largest piece of land. They sat down around a fire and were cooking some of the leftover buffalo meat from the other day.

"So, Gabbin..." said Forky, mouth full, chewing on a buffalo sandwich, "you know we have to take the treasure from a terrible monster, right?"

Bobill looked at him and answered, "Ummmm, Randolf is gone forever... don't you Dorks even give a care?"

Forky then said, "He'll be back, he always comes back!"

Bobill just cried loudly for a few hours. When he was done, he said to Forky, "You were saying earlier?"

Forky shot a mysterious glance at Bobill and spoke in a hushed tone. "This rhyme..." he said, eyes gleaming, "is how people know him.

> *'He is the greatest creature of all,*
> *with his razor claws.*
> *Even the bravest knights will fall,*
> *before his iron jaws.*
> *With eyes like the dawn,*
> *and breath of flame,*
> *he rules over all the land,*
> *I will not fail to mention his name:*
> *Domardacktilianofarjenseriumsan.'*

We have to kill a one-thousand-foot-long Dragon to get back the treasure of old."

Bobill took a deep breath; he didn't think he would make it back to his cozy little mud hole.

"Well, I suppose I'll sleep well tonight!" Bobill said with absolute sarcasm.

He knew he shouldn't have been surprised. Randolf had mentioned a probability of having to slay foul creatures way back when he first met him, and that they would almost certainly all be killed at least several times throughout the trip. Actually, now that Bobill thought of it, the word 'Dragon' may have even been tossed around without him paying any heed to it at the time. But why would he have? He'd never really believed Dragons were real, they were just storybook nonsense, and one would have to be a real nutcase to want to take the time to read a fictional book about made-up characters traveling across fake lands to slay a non-existent Dragon. At least that's what he was thinking anyway. But Forky sounded pretty sure and was moderately convincing; now he wasn't sure what to believe.

So, the sad little Gabbin cast himself down, got semi-comfortable, and went to sleep. That night, he dreamt of Randolf, falling and screaming and calling for help, and saying,

"Stop dreaming about me, you weirdo!"

The next morning the Dorks were singing so loud that Bobill had to hold his ears. Even worse, they were doing that running thing again, but over old bridges this time. They reached the last and longest bridge, and halfway over it, they met a mean-looking man with wispy, wild gray hair, a long, frizzled beard, and a two-foot-wide, stick-straight mustache. He was wearing tattered, faded clothes, and looked as if he hadn't left that spot in years.

He narrowed his suspicious purple eyes and spoke unto them. "Pay yer toll, and ye shall pass. It's"—he paused and counted them under his breath—"$15.75."

But Jerky protested, "That doesn't split up evenly six ways!"

The mean man's expression hardened at this, then he pointed a long, crooked finger at Porky. "That one costs extry! And ye *must've* fergott'n the *included* county tax and bridge restoration fund. Ye thinks it cost nothin' to maintain these crossins after fatbutts like yerselves keep a-stamping across 'em?"

With sighs and grumbles all around, the Dorks and Bobill emptied their pockets and sockets, but they only managed to come up with $15.74. The man immediately drew out a huge battle-axe from who knows where.

"If ye can't pay tha whole toll, then ye shall fight me to tha death!"

The Dorks pushed the Gabbin up to the man. "*He* is a master of the fighting arts!" said Forky, referring to Bobill.

The mean-looking man leaned in and gave Bobill the 'one-eyed look'.

Bobill thought to himself, *"This is my chance!"*

He unsheathed his finger and poked him right in his

eye. The mean-looking man clapped a hand over the eye, yelling and flailing his free arm all around. Bobill innocently stuck out his long shoe right behind the man's wildly dancing legs, causing him to somehow lose his balance and fall screaming to his doom.

"Say hello to Randolf for me, JERK!!!" screamed Bobill.

Feeling quite proud of himself, Bobill looked up to study the Dorks' reaction to his latest victory, but they were gone. Up ahead, he saw dust rising. They had passed around him and ran away. Bobill tried catching up with them, but it was just about hopeless. The Dorks were out of sight.

Chapter 10:
Shadow of the Mountain

Bobill had finally left Bread Ridges behind and was now in a wide, green field with mossy boulders lying here and there. There was a small stream of cool, clear water for him to drink and fill up his tiny bottles with. He just now noticed that he could see the Mountain of Solitude ahead, towering over the horizon like a tall, pointy, rocky triangle. He knew the Dorks would be headed that way, so he told himself he wouldn't hurry to catch up.

Nevertheless, he needed to make some progress, so he got up and continued on. He climbed over hills and rocks, finding obvious clues all over the place that the Dorks had been there. Then he saw it. A trail of blood leading over to a short cluster of trees on his left side. He clapped his hands over his mouth to stifle a scream but kept creeping forward cautiously.

The red splatters went over a hill with a few little bushes and rocks on top, an ideal place for Bobill to sneak up to and peek down at the area ahead.

The trail ended on the edge of the patch of trees, and it was unmistakable that there were animals gathered and feasting there. He tip-toed closer, using any weeds or shrubs to take quick cover behind. He was close enough now to see it was not *many* creatures, as he had thought, but one. He could also make out what the creature was.

"Saber-toothed timber moose," whispered Bobill to himself, shuddering at the sight of the massive beast.

A regular moose was bad enough, especially to someone Bobill's size, but a saber-toothed timber moose was something else entirely. It was nearly twice the size of its normal counterpart, and its gigantic antlers were razor-sharp for slicing. It also had very large, pointy teeth for cutting and tearing prey made of meats, with two extra-long fangs in the front... earning it the name. Several thousand pounds it must've been, for Bobill could feel the very ground tremble with every small step it made, shifting its enormous bulk as it chowed down on something. Of course, Bobill knew what that something was.... It was... his acquaintances.

This was confirmed when he saw Corky's red, pointy hat, even more red now, hanging from the side of the beast's mouth. His heart sank. He hated this quest and everything about it. Though he really couldn't stand the Dorks, he didn't wish this on them. But he figured their reckless behavior and lack of caution would inevitably lead them to such an end. He was now completely alone in the wilderness and wasn't quite sure what to do. He could try going back home, but he would have to go far around Bread Ridges now that the bridges were gone, and possibly back through Kirkwoods.

After a while of thinking, he decided to move on. If he was going to perish all by himself in these strange lands, he would like to at least see if he could take a peek at the supposedly non-fictional treasure he came all this way for. He put a look of determination on his face, tightened his wig, rolled up his socks, and marched on toward the mountain. After three or seven steps, he was halted when everything around him began to shake vigorously.

"Oh no..." he said to himself in terror.

He turned quickly, and laid eyes on what he feared to be true. The saber-toothed timber moose was barreling in on him like an avalanche of furry, greasy, bloody, antlered rage. Bobill could barely keep his feet planted, but he spun around and sprinted as hard as he could. There was no way he could outrun it; he had to find somewhere to hide. The little Gabbin swerved to the left sharply, back to the cluster of trees. The heavy thudding hooves and tremendous snorting were closing in fast.

"AAHHH!!!" Bobill suddenly and involuntarily

squealed, as he dove at the first tree he came to.

'SLAM!' He hit the tree full force, nearly knocking himself out.

He held it together and scrambled upward like a crazed orangutan, still screaming maniacally. When he reached the very top, he noticed he was just about even with the timber moose's mouth. He continued screaming and leapt off the treetop. Just as his feet left it, the timber moose bit down on the tree, uprooted it, and threw it about five hundred feet away. Bobill caught a low branch of another tree nearby and began fighting through the boughs on his way to the top. He didn't have time to catch his breath before his new branchy haven was shaking all over the place.

The timber moose was shredding the base of the tree apart with its antlers like a hundred freshly sharpened machetes. But this tree was thankfully much thicker than the last; it wouldn't go down so easily. Bobill held tight for what seemed like hours while violently shaking, swaying, and jolting around.

Then he heard it... 'Crack, crackle, CRACK!!' The tree was beginning to fall.

He immediately let go and slid down the tree, trying desperately to avoid the incoming branches.

Right when the tree landed with a thunderous 'KUH-

RAASH!!!' Bobill tucked and rolled onto the ground as well.

He slowly sat up, barely able to move. The tree and some of its major limbs had missed him narrowly, but he now found his nose only inches away from the timber moose's jaws. The rotten breath was more than Bobill could take. He covered his mouth, barfed, and swallowed it down smooth. Now, all he could do was wait to be devoured. He was too tired to do anything else. The timber moose sniffed at him, then stepped forward and right over him, still sniffing.

"What in the frigging daggone heck is he doing?" thought Bobill.

The sniffing sound trailed off, as did the thumping and rumbling of the hooves.

"Guess he's not hungry," Bobill mumbled to himself.

Just then, he noticed something... a shiny object, seemingly on his hand, one could even say his finger. It was rounded in shape, and cool to the touch like some sort of metal....

"The RING!" he cried.

He had forgotten all about it. It must have slipped on when he fell. It certainly would've made this whole encounter much easier. The timber moose couldn't even see him. Bobill breathed deep and sat awhile, regaining some of his strength before eventually setting out once more. He made sure he was far away from that horrid beast before he finally removed the ring and flipped it high in the air, opening his pocket for it to fall into. It missed. He picked it up, and with a fading grin, he tried several more times before it slipped in silently at last.

All at once, he closed his eyes, bit his lip, made a fist, and pumped his arm twice in a celebratory fashion. He would have to make sure he remembered that magical circle in the future. On the way out of the timber moose's domain, he grabbed Corky's hat and stuffed it in his fanny pack for remembrance.

Bobill had been traveling for many hours now, still trying to reach the mountain. The sun was getting low in the sky, and he felt none too comfortable still being out here without any help. The weird nightly noises of the wild were starting up already, and he wondered if the timber moose would track him down and try to eat him again. Exhaustion was setting in fiercely, he had to get out of the open and find somewhere safe to sleep for the night. He soon wouldn't be able to see well enough to do so, much less continue moving forward. He began to explore off to his right side, taking care not to venture too far into the thicker wooded areas. He made his way to a large grassy hill, and as he approached, he found that one side had a flat, rocky wall, and a small crack was discovered there that he could climb into with ease.

It was like a small room inside, not going any deeper than what he could tell. After a thorough search, he figured he'd be just fine in there for the night. He flopped down on the cool, damp floor, and drifted off into a deep, snoring sleep. When he awoke the next morning, it was bright and sunny outside... except it wasn't at all. It was pitch black dark, and still plenty nightly out. He sat up quickly in fright when he heard some rustling sounds outside. Staying very still, he listened carefully. Nothing at all for a while until... more rustling, and... voices. The sounds were close, right at the opening.

"Yesss, this shall make quite the nice snack!" Bobill heard someone suddenly say.

Bobill pulled out his sword Stink and stood to his feet, aiming the cold steel at the crack and ready to rain down some pointy vengeance. It was then he realized that he had forgotten about his sword too! He had it all this time, yet he'd been striking down foes with musical instruments made from rocks instead. What a fool he had been; but now, he was prepared. He'd carve up these intruders if it was the last thing he did. Just then, multiple dark figures stepped in through the opening.

"In the name of my grandpappy Jobill! I will smite you

savages where you stand!" bellowed Bobill, as he flung himself at his attackers, swinging Stink wildly.

There were sparks flashing, metal clattering, things banging, and much screaming. Bobill swung harder and faster, and when he was sure he had cut the evil beings to ribbons, he stopped and let his arms drop to his sides, panting and sweating profusely.

He still couldn't see very well, but good enough to carefully step over the bodies that lie in ruin from his ferocious onslaught. He crept out and briskly trotted away from the little cave, back to the open fields that ran down toward the mountain.

It wasn't long before the first light of dawn came. Bobill didn't feel like he'd gotten much rest, but he needed to get out of here, to somewhere he could feel truly safe and secure. He kept going after reaching the clearings again, and after only a short walk, he came across a large, ancient, fallen tree across his path ahead. It was around ten feet thick but very long, so he attempted to struggle his way over it. He rubbed his hands together and slowly climbed up, fingertips digging into the old, rotten bark. When he reached the top (or side), he slipped and fell forward, arms flailing helplessly.

'Thud!' He crumpled into something soft, and that something proceeded to let out a blood-curdling "aaAAAHHH!!!"

Bobill rolled off of it and went for his sword, but upon seeing what it was, he stopped, mouth open wide in pure shock.

"Porky!!" yelled Bobill. "I thought you were dead!"

Porky shouted back. "We thought you were dead too!"

Only then did Bobill notice the other Dorks were right there as well: Corky, Jerky, Slerky, and Forky Rottenfield, all huddled tight to the giant tree. Bobill pulled out Corky's bloody cone-hat and handed it to him.

"I found this a ways back, being chewed on by a saber-toothed timber moose," said Bobill. "There was blood sprayed everywhere! So much that I was sure it had gotten you all."

Corky sucked his teeth and said, "This ain't blood, you goof. That stupid moose brute blindsided us and swiped the hat right off my head. Under my hat is where I keep my emergency one-gallon jar of pickled tomato sauce. When it started tearing into the stuff, we took off and got the heck out of there."

Jerky then added, "We figured you died fighting that mean guy on the bridge. We even said a few touching and kind words about you—shoulda heard us."

Bobill was quite annoyed, and rightfully so.

"You Dorks thought I'd lose to the bridge meanie, so you ran away?!" he cried angrily.

Slerky began to say something but closed his mouth.

Forky then stood, and in a nearly sincere tone, said to Bobill, "We are quite sorry, Master Gabbin. It appears you may be able to handle yourself after all." Bobill rolled his eyes, and Forky continued, "We surely could use your... *expertise* now. Not too far back, we ran into some trouble. We were trying to find a place to sleep last night when some kind of insane creature attacked us at the entrance of a small cave. It swung a pointy, silver stick at us and screamed like a deranged demon. We dropped our sleeping bags right there and hauled buns all the way here. We were just now drawing straws to see who would go back and get the equipment. Maybe you could sneak over and grab our things."

Bobill was absolutely furious now. After all he had been through, now they wanted him to immediately risk his life against some unearthly demon just to get their *stuff*? At the same time, he was glad to have company again... dimwitted and irritating as they were. Besides, he was keeping track of how much they owed him for all of the constant saving of their lives he was doing. This would be easy anyway, he would just slip the ring on, grab the stuff, and get right back to them; no need to confront the insane cave demon.

That's just what he did; he backtracked to where they said their belongings were, put on the ring, and strolled into the area unseen. There was a rock face with a small crack in it, opening up into a room of sorts. Inside, scattered all around the entrance, were all of the Dorks' sleeping bags of various shapes and colors. He gathered them up, not daring to peer into the darkness of the cave, and ran back to the Dorks. When he was nearly there, he kicked the ring off with his shoe as he was running, and it flipped into his pocket. He climbed back over the fallen tree and slid down the other side.

"Got them!" he said.

But they were not there. He looked toward the mountain to see them all running away again.

"GOOD BLEEPING GRIEF!!" screamed Bobill, seething with rage.

He slammed the bags down in the dirt and took off after them. He pushed himself hard, determined to keep up this time. Slowly but surely, after a good while of sprinting, Bobill had almost reached them. Forky was out front, legs flying high and palms flattened for speed. Behind him in a row, were Porky, Jerky, Slerky, and finally, Corky, who seemed to be the slowest by a small margin.

Through his panting and puffing, Bobill called out, "SLOW DOWN, YOU DORKS!!"

The Dorks instantly stopped dead, but Bobill could not. He slammed into Corky just as he was turning around to reply. Bobill slid up over Corky, flipping end over end across all of the Dorks' heads. Bobill landed in a patch of soft shallow gravel and slid ten or fifty feet on his teeth through it, then he came to a smoking halt.

Jerky came jogging up to the wreckage, looked at him, and said, "Doin' okay there, Bo?"

Bobill burned with anger. "Don't EVER call me that! And NO, I'm not doing '*okay*', I've been chasing you dumb Dorks this entire journey... I'm sick of it!!!"

Jerky and the other Dorks just sat there staring.

Then Corky said to Bobill, "I didn't know you felt that way about us. We'll try not to run too fast for you anymore... Bo." Bobill socked Corky between his eyes and walked away for a moment. He came back and eyed Forky closely.

"Took off again because you thought the insane cave demon would surely get me, huh?" snapped Bobill, poking Forky in the chest. "Well, I've got news for you simpletons. I've basically defeated every single opponent you've come across and then some! I think I deserve some recognition! To at least not have to worry about being left behind!"

The Dorks looked down, ashamed of their selfish ways.

Forky sighed and said, "You're right. We wouldn't have made it ten miles without you on this trip. Perhaps we've been blinded by greed—the desire of the lost treasure that is calling to us.... But no more! We shall unite, and we shall travel and fight together as one!"

As he finished, with one fist in the air as a sign of absolution, he outstretched his hand toward Bobill. Bobill glanced down at the five digits that patiently waited for embrace. Then, quick as lightning, he cast ropes around all of the Dorks, pulling tight and watching them drop to the ground. While laughing hysterically, he tied them all up and drug them through jagged rocks, mud, streams, and sand for about thirty miles. Finally, he stopped and untied them when he reached a large, strange sign surrounded by weeds. The Dorks slowly got up and brushed the rocks and dirt off themselves as Bobill took a look at what was written on the sign.

'Weclome to CakeTown' it read.

"Well, they spelled 'welcome' wrong, hope that doesn't mean that we *aren't*," said Bobill. "I think you Dorks have possibly learned a lesson or two—it's all in the past now. Let's move forward, maybe stock up on some cake in this town, and get ourselves up that mountain."

The Dorks nodded, and as they all began to leave, they heard a quiet 'thump' behind them. Forky walked up to the back of the town sign and found that the noise was just one of the old letters that had fallen off onto the ground. No doubt from them looking at it so much. Forky shook his head and didn't even bother picking the big faded 'C' up.

"We'll have to tell someone they need to fix their junky sign when we get there," he mumbled.

Then he rejoined the group and they headed onward again. After proceeding around a thick patch of woods to their right, they saw the town before them, not at all too far away. It lay just a short distance from the base of the Mountain of Solitude beyond. They had traveled 1,487 miles from Bobill's mud hole.

"We made it!" yelled Forky.

Chapter 11:
Of Cardboard & Keyhole

Bobill and the Dorks had ever-widening smiles on their faces as they approached the town. It looked perfectly splendid. There were great wooden halls, houses, shops, restaurants, and folk out in the streets laughing and carrying on joyously. They could taste the cakes already. The only problem was, there was a previously unseen river of water between them and the town. It had apparently been obscured by the smooth hill that they were walking over.

The Solitary River it was, for it ran down from the mountain itself, wound around the town, and eventually fell into a mist off the edge of Bread Ridges downstream. Here the river was a few hundred feet wide at least, and very deep. The group would have to find some kind of boat or raft to get across. The Dorks got to work chopping down some decently thick trees, while Bobill began lashing them together with the rope he had used to tie up the Dorks.

Before long, they had themselves a seaworthy vessel. Forky took the helm on the upper deck. Porky took command of the galley and mess hall below the main deck, although they had no food for cooking whatsoever. Jerky took to the crow's nest as a lookout for pirates, while Slerky and Corky handled the rigging and sails. Finally, Bobill was given a mop and bucket to swab the poop deck.

They shoved off, starting from further upstream so they wouldn't have to fight the current as much as they would going straight across. There was an unhappy wind in the air over the river of water that day, and they had a fair share of difficulty keeping the makeshift raft together on the voyage. Only through sheer bravery and determination did they land safely at last on the far shore... seven minutes after they had set sail. They dropped anchor, hoping to possibly use the vessel again at some point. Then the little sailors all filed one by one down the ramp onto dry land once more.

It was only a short walk from the boat to CakeTown, and the group was anxious to see if the local residents would be considerate enough to help them out. The town was somewhat large and was built upon what seemed to be an enormous porch. All of the buildings, roads, alleys, mailboxes, benches, light posts, and parking meters within were made of wood as if they were all one giant, single structure. The porch was raised on thick and strong beams underneath, thrust deep into the viscous mud below the entire town.

The group spied a wide stairway that ascended up to the porch level, so they took to it, climbing up to see what awaited them. They stuck together, and walked down the main street of the town, passing several establishments of goods and services. There were fancy, decorative and colorful names painted boldly on the front each and every one. CakeTown Bakery, of course; CakeTown Butcher Shop, CakeTown General Goods, CakeTown Barber, CakeTown Police Station... you get the idea.

Many people were milling about the place; workers and shopkeepers, guards and civilians, all chatting away and smiling as if they didn't have a care in the world. Bobill however, and soon the Dorks as well, noticed that something was wrong. They heard... nothing. There was no chatting, no sounds of workers or machines. It was dead quiet except for the breeze softly rustling between the buildings and wooden boards. The group stopped in their tracks, very concerned. None of these townfolk were moving at all. They seemed to be frozen in time. After a few moments, Jerky took in a deep breath and decided he would go up to one of them to see just what their problem was. He moved slowly, easing his way up to a tall lady sporting wavy, light brown hair and wearing a long, blue dress.

She looked to be in the middle of laughing at a joke, eyes

mostly closed and mouth wide open; though there was really no one quite close enough to have caused such a reaction. Jerky examined her from a few feet away, then pulled out his axe, flipped it around with the end of the handle facing the woman, and lightly thrust it forward. To his horror, the handle easily punched right through her belly with a ripping sound, light showing through the hole as he recoiled the weapon. Jerky stepped back and began panicking.

Bobill and the other Dorks had advanced a little to the point where they too saw what happened. A few of them were just about to run away, but before they got the chance, the woman fell to the wooden sidewalk, staying perfectly stiff the whole way down. They now saw that she was almost completely flat, as if she were made out of a board of cardpaper. Jerky leaned in again for a better look and discovered that she indeed was not real at all, but rather a realistically painted image. At the base of the counterfeit woman, a tab had broken off that was still inserted into a slot cut into the wood below for holding her upright. Who or what could have done this, and to what purpose, none of them could guess. There they stood, looking all around themselves at the now much less pleasant place when they heard a 'clack!' to their left, coming from a storefront.

Forky headed over to the noise, axe in hand, inspecting the area. Bobill saw him drop to a knee, and as he stood and turned to face the rest of them, he held up something. It was a thin, square piece of wood, and upon one side was painted a big, bright-yellow letter 'C'; it had fallen from above. Bobill looked up at the storefront to where it came from. It had been the first letter in the word 'CakeTown', but now, where the 'C' once stood, was a big fat 'F'.

"FakeTown?" asked Bobill to no one in particular.

"What is this madness?" growled Forky, dropping the piece of wood as he warily surveyed his surroundings. "We haven't got time to play games. Something is not right with this place. If it's supposed to be some kind of joke, I'm certainly not laughing. Let's search the place and see if there's anything worth taking—there doesn't seem to be anyone here to claim ownership anyway."

They remained close and systematically searched each building. On more than one occasion, a few of them had caught a glimpse of what looked like something moving very quickly in the shadows, darting between buildings and across rooftops. It was brushed off as nothing more than tricks of the mind due to being in such an eerie place. Obviously, nobody could live here in such isolation without food or supplies, right? They ignored the illusions and proceeded, shoving aside false, flat cardboard people left and right and thoroughly rummaging through every drawer and cabinet. Alas, they found naught but paintings of food and drink on cardboard and walls...

The group exited the last shop on the main street, coming finally to the largest building in town which sat at the end of the road. They walked up the stairs, across the sizeable, roofed front porch, and pushed open the double doors with a loud 'creeaaak'.

They studied the interior a while and saw that it was some kind of important building for meetings of sorts. There were four rows of pews stretching up to the front, with some high seats behind thick desks near the far wall facing back at them. All at once, they noticed the painfully obvious; there, front and center, under a beam of light shining in through a circular window in the roof, was a round, wooden table.

On that table lay a bright pink cake big enough to cover the table's entire surface, which was maybe three feet or so. Forky turned around to the rest of the group behind him and chuckled.

"Like we would be stupid enough to fall for—" he stopped short, seeing the wide-eyed terror on the faces of the group who seemed to be looking right past him.

All of them... except for Porky. The Dork had slipped around Forky as he was turning and ran for the cake.

Forky quickly spun around and lurched forward, arms

outstretched and screaming, "NO, PORKY!!"

But it was too late. A rope on the floor tightened around Porky's ankles, which were still sore from when Bobill had tied him up. He fell flat, cake all over his hands, nose, and beard.

A loud 'ZIP!' was heard as he took off across the room, wrapping around poles, going up and down walls, over and under the pews, and coming at last to rest in front of the large middle desk, not far from where he started.

Before he could do or say anything, a panel opened on the front of the desk. Porky shot inside a dark passage in the blink of an eye and the panel slammed shut. The other Dorks sprang into action, running up to the panel and hacking it apart with their axes. Bobill stood behind them with Stink unsheathed, ready for stabbing. With a mighty final blow, Forky obliterated the secret wooden door. The group was met with a dark, musty, stone stairway, vanishing steeply downward into a black void. Slerky and Jerky quickly whipped together some cloth and broken boards for a few torches, then they all began their descent.

A bunch of minutes after walking down cold, damp steps, Bobill and the Dorks reached the bottom. The passage continued straight through a long, unchanging hall; the floor, walls, and ceiling above were all made of stone. Eventually, they reached a sharp right turn. Forky crept up to the corner, put one hand on the stone wall, then hastily leaned head and torch around it to see. Almost instantly, he threw himself back with a cry, torch flipping through the air and landing several feet away. All the others gripped their weapons and moved up to assist.

"What was it?" asked Corky in a loud whisper.

Forky did not meet his gaze but answered him shakily. "A face. A twisted, rotting corpse-like face that hissed at me and shambled off into the blackness."

Bobill shuddered, as the rest of them most likely did. The description reminded him of the creature he had riddled with in the caves before and gotten the ring from. The ring... he wished he could put it on now. It would be so easy to check things out down here without being attacked, but something inside told him not to let the Dorks know of its existence just yet. It was quite a strange thing indeed, and he feared what others may think of his ownership of it. For now, he put it out of his mind; he knew he must push on and help to find their missing companion. Bobill walked to the front where Forky still lay crumpled to the floor in shock. He grabbed Forky by the arm and yanked him to his feet.

"Come on," Bobill said to him before turning to the rest. "All of you. Let's rush in swinging and strike them down! We have to get Porky out of this dreadful place."

Nods and grunts of agreement all around.

"Alright," said Forky, coming to his senses, "let's do this."

The group synced up, turned the corner, and sprinted down the next hallway. Their weapons were outstretched ahead of each one of them, begging for an evil hide to pierce. The hall suddenly opened up into a large chamber and the group slid to a stop. Dim lamps were scattered around, illuminating small areas that the group's own torches could not entirely reach. They could see what looked to be toilets all over the sides of the room, apparently as a stand-in for any and all furniture here. There was a row of them together making a couch, a raised toilet for a sink, a toilet with parallel, metal bars spanning its top to make a grill, and lastly, a regular toilet for toiletizing in.

Without warning, a shadowy, thin figure slunk out from the thin shadows. It was human-like in shape and wore shabby, off-brand rags. Soon after, more things like it crawled out from little crevices, doorways, and tunnels in the walls and floor. All of them, thirty or so, gathered to the center of the room and menacingly faced the group. It was only then that Bobill and the Dorks noticed the net suspended from the dark ceiling containing their poor, captured friend. The lead stranger stepped forward and removed the mask he was wearing. It revealed a fairly less hideous face underneath, though admittedly he would certainly not be winning any beauty contests. He, like the rest of those amongst him, looked to be malnourished and pale; undoubtedly, they did not get out much. He also had very little hair, and presumably tried to make it less noticeable by gluing a folded, gray sock to the top of his head.

Once the leader revealed himself, he brandished a long, dirty, crooked, rusty knife, and spoke to the group in a harsh tone. "Give us your supplies, and we may let you live."

Forky also took a step forward and answered him. "Cut our friend down now, or you shall taste our blades. I must warn you, they haven't been sharpened in a while, so we may have to do some sawing."

The lead stranger hissed, stepping even closer now, then replied, "I am Gourden, Governor of FakeTown and what people it has left. You have trespassed on *our* porch, the porch of a people starving and terrified of a winged dragenoid that haunts yonder mountain. You will give us *ALL* of your provisions, or your tubby chum will soon be relieved of his innards."

Gourden cocked his head, and without breaking his stare at Forky, called to someone behind him. "Clumbette!"

A young female person stepped out from the crowd,

removing her ghastly face covering and letting brown, tangled hair drop to her mid-back. Her dark eyes pierced right through Bobill and the Dorks with a hateful glare.

"Grab the Gutspon and ready it to the captive's flubby breadbasket," said Gourden.

Clumbette quickly produced a huge spoon, five feet in length, with a wickedly sharp, serrated edge.

Gourden's expression did not change, but he said now to Forky, "The Gutspon was forged for one purpose... but we use it for something else: scooping clean the bodies of those who dare oppose us."

Forky, feeling he had no other option, tightened the grip of his axe and prepared to lunge at Gourden. Gourden lifted his hand as if he were about to give the signal to scoop.

Things got really tense, and just as all heck was about to break loose, a little voice cried out, "Stop, you morons!!"

It was Bobill.

"We have no provisions, Mister Governor sir. We were hoping to find some here on our way to slay the Dragon within the mountain and retrieve the loads of gold that he guards. So *much* gold in fact, that we PROBABLY COULDN'T EVEN CARRY IT ALL WITH US WHEN WE LEAVE!" Bobill's voice raised loudly towards the end of his statement while he winked rapidly.

"Killing the dragenoid, say you? Too much to carry, was it?" inquired Gourden rhetorically with great interest.

Forky nodded reluctantly, followed by the other Dorks.

Gourden snapped his boney fingers and said, "Stow the Gutspon, Clumbette. The situation has taken a turn, and we now have some... matters... to discuss."

Everyone slowly sheathed their weaponry, suspicion still in many eyes. Gourden motioned for the group to sit down on the toilet couch and pulled up a toilet to sit upon.

"You must attempt to disregard our humble sittery," he said, in a far more polite manner. "You see, we came here several years ago, without knowledge of yon dragenoid. We raised the mighty porch from out of the muck below and built upon it a promising little town. But alas, just before things really got going, we were attacked. We know not why he spared us his furious flamery, but swoop down and catch many of us he did. We tried in vain to fight the heckspawn off—invincible he seemed to be. He eventually retreated back to his abode, and we quickly got to work digging this passage. The only thing we ever came out to do was set up cardboard cutouts of townsfolk for luring in unsuspecting travelers to take their goods. It was for that reason we called it FakeTown, since we never had time to properly name the place—but after we couldn't seem to capture anyone, we slapped some 'C's over the signs to make the far more attractive sounding 'CakeTown'."

He shifted uneasily on his toilet. "It was, unfortunately, the only way we could survive probably. It only took the dragenoid one look at the place full of fake persons to forsake it as abandoned, yet we still fear to come up, for he is quick, and we want not for him to know of our hiding place here.... However, your arrival now heralds new hope for our town's future if what you say is true *and* can really be done."

Forky nodded for a minute, taking it all in. Then he said, "So what's the deal with all the toilets exactly? I was waiting for that part in the story."

Gourden scrunched his eyebrows a bit and sighed, giving a slight chuckle. "The Elf King of Kirkwoods and his host were passing through here a few weeks after the attack on the town. When I peered out and saw them, I decided to risk coming out and asking for help. Evidently, they had recently installed all new bathrooms throughout the entire secret KirkElf kingdom and were looking for a place to get rid of their old toilets. So, when I pleaded for food and protection for my people, the king smiled, dumped a massive pile of toilets all over the ground in front of me, and quietly rode away. I'll never forget the last thing he said to me as he faded into the distance. I called out, begging to him, 'We shall surely perish without your aid, good King!' and he simply replied, 'Ha!' and turned away. So, these toilets are now some of our only possessions."

Forky looked satisfied now, though troubled at the news previously unknown to him: Elves living in Kirkwoods, who likely would've shot his beard off had they crossed paths there.

"Alright then," said Forky. "Let us strike a deal."

Gourden and Forky finished their bargaining, which consisted of only the two statements: 'Kill the dragenoid and give us some gold', and 'Okay'. You can decide which was spoken by whom.

"By the way," said Gourden, "this is Clumbette, my daughter, Vice Governor, and heir to the porcelain throne. We haven't much to offer, as you can see, but if you need anything that doesn't involve us coming out of this bunker, do not hesitate to ask it of us. Unless it's something really stupid and annoying. Go now with our blessing, to yon mountain."

With that, they finally cut Porky down and unbound him.

"That cake wasn't real," he said.

Up they climbed around the back of the mountain, avoiding the plain and obvious front entrance that would mean certain death. Hundreds of feet straight up they went, digging their fingernails into the smooth rock. They almost died only a few times along the way, and when they got near the top, they discovered a small, flat ledge on which they could all comfortably stand. Forky told Bobill that he was sure this area was in fact the location of a super-secretive hidden door.

"My late father, Florkus, designed the door as an emergency exit," he said. "What would he say if only he could see me now, back at the very doors of the treasure heap! He entrusted me with *this* in his final years."

He produced a key that was shaped like a mountain with a Dragon inside laying on a pile of treasure.

"The only time this key will work is when the door appears," said Forky. "It only appears when it's partly cloudy and seventy-eight degrees outside with sixty percent humidity. I think all the planets in the universe have to be lined up too. Also, you have to say a magical word the moment the event happens—which I forgot—so we'll have to guess. We'll only have ten seconds after the door shows up to figure out the word that reveals the keyhole."

Just then, they heard a 'boop' sound.

It was the secret door popping up on the mountainside. Everyone started shouting out passwords at the door.

It ended up being 'Cheesewinkle', which Bobill guessed with great pride.

'Wayyeeeowww!' was the sound that occurred when the keyhole appeared.

Forky jammed that key into the hole and turned it with force. The great door creaked open, and just behind was a tunnel with darkness in it. Forky then told Bobill to go in and look around.

"We've got your little back, Bobill," he said with a semi-assuring grin. "We'll guard this entrance with our very lives. All you have to do is some of that magical sneaking nonsense you seem to be so good at. Then come back and give us the details of what we'll be working with down there."

Bobill complained for a few minutes, but after Forky seized him by his fanny pack and cast him inside, he went on down the long tunnel to certain doom.

Chapter 12:
Domard's Lair

Bobill hesitantly moved forward down the dark and secret tunnel that had been bored through the back of the mountain. During this time, he thought about all he had been through with the Dorks. He thought of Randolf and hoped that he may yet still live. After all, he *had* been the one that spoke of the possibility of pillows at the bottom of Bread Ridges. He wished the unstable geriatric were here with him now. Surely that old Wizard would know how to deal with a Dragon far better than poor little Bobill.

The Dragon... now all his thought fixed upon it. He had never seen one, and quite believed they did not exist. The fellow had witnessed, escaped, and even defeated many strange and fearsome creatures throughout this journey. But if the Dragon was anything like the stories he'd heard when he was but a young Gabbin, there was nothing any of them could hope to do against it. Defeating Dragons was the work of armies of Elf warriors or immortal beings sent from the lands beyond, not fat little baby-men who just want to have a nice sit-down and a cup of tea with buttercakes. The whole idea made his head spin, but he was able to harness his fears when he remembered a certain circular object that he possessed.

Yes, of course... he would slip on that ring of his, get a good eyeful of the place, Dragon or nay, and come back to the Dorks a hero. What would come after that, he did not know. But in his mind, this journey was finally nearing its end. He would be able to go home soon and get back to a frightfully busy schedule of doing absolutely nothing. Besides, Dragons probably didn't exist anyway....

The straight and narrow passage had at last opened up into a gigantic room. There was a very small amount of hazy light coming from an unseen source. Whether by magic, natural causes, or just easier storytelling, Bobill was certainly unsure. He could just barely make out the shape of the place inside, but one thing was undeniable: *many* treasures lie in this room; heaping piles of golden shinies were scattered all around the place. There were chests on top chests lining the walls, overflowing with untold and fabulous riches.

Enormous pillars held up the high ceiling above, one hundred feet and half again perhaps; he couldn't tell exactly, it was dark and uninteresting up there. The entire room seemed to slope or stairstep downward from all sides into a lower center floor. Before he took note of even one more thing, Bobill grasped the ring in his pocket, set it on his left thumbnail, and flipped it several feet into the air. It plummeted down, flipping end over end, increasing its speed with every inch. With complete silence, the ring slipped over Bobill's chubby, right middle finger. He'd been aiming for his pointer, but what did it matter, it obviously fit that finger just as well. It was entirely possible that the ring had a mystical stretchiness to it or some such.

With the ring now on, he could see the room much better, although that wasn't normally the case when wearing it. He was quite puzzled by this, as he also noticed shadows being cast outward from his position. Something just above him was glowing brightly. He quickly pulled a small mirror out of his fanny pack that he sometimes used to see how amazing he believed he looked. He held it outstretched and tilted the top back a bit to see what was over his head. To his great surprise and horror, his wig was glowing with intense brightness. He hurriedly yanked the ring off his finger, and the light was instantly extinguished. He allowed his heart to slow again, though it proved difficult. He was nearly sure he had heard something rustling about somewhere in the room while his headlight was on.

Carefully, he slid the ring on to his pointer finger this time and knew now that he had indeed gone comfortably into sweet unseeableness. With relief in his bones, he moved on down the sloping stairs littered with pointy jewels and slippery coins. The floor leveled out as he reached the wide expanse at the bottom of the room. Though he wasn't visible, he paid close attention to the small piles of gold here and there, trying desperately not to topple any of them over. He had seen no trace of any living thing so far, but he couldn't be too careful. There were many areas out of his line of sight that could contain a large, hideous, winged, fire-breathing killing machine.

He approached the first pillar to his left and examined the various trinkets and whatsits surrounding its base. He scanned around to the right side and... he bit his lip, stifling a shriek. There it was... the Dragon itself staring menacingly into Bobill's eyes. It *was* real after all! Could it see him? Did it have some power greater than that of his ring with which to pierce through its trickery? The horned head and gaping jaws did not move, but neither did Bobill. As he squinted his beady eyes in the darkness, he could now see it was only a big Dragon statue made of gold.

"OH!" he exclaimed. "Oh, thank cheese." He walked up to the statue and flicked it on the nose with a light chuckle.

He knew Dragons weren't real.

Just then, he saw a thing that he could not believe had gone unnoticed until this moment. In the open mouth of the statue was held an immense, gold-plated meteor, a very rare item indeed. Bobill grabbed the dazzling rock and shoved it straight into his fanny pack, filling it almost to bursting. The Dorks would flip their lids when they saw this prize. By this time, he was confident he'd searched the place well enough to know that no super-sized lizard of any kind could possibly be inside it, so he made for the exit.

After only a few steps, however, there came a thing of concern. A thick, heavy, clear, liquid substance splashed on the floor at his feet. Bobill began to tremble. He glanced up in time to see an unbelievably long, shadowy shape slowly and quietly slide along the ceiling to one of the far pillars. Like a snake that heeds not things like gravity, it slithered off the ceiling and onto the pillar, coiling around as it descended. Bobill started walking again, quickening his pace with every step now. He heard the unmistakable sound of coins jingling in the distance and knew that the thing was on the floor. As he sped up to nearly a jog, the long, dark thing had encircled the entire room, passing Bobill on his right, then thrusting forth its head directly in front of Bobill's way out.

The creature's head, topped with twisted horns, raised up from the floor. Its nostrils flared, sniffing the room, and its yellow eyes narrowed, scanning over every inch of its lair. One of its huge claws slammed down hard, only several feet further and Bobill would've been paste. Bobill saw now the jagged scales which covered the entirety of its body, dark greenish, neon brown-silver in hue, like a tremendous, slick and slippery river fish... with horns and claws. Bobill could still hear its tail whipping around in the loose gold far away behind him. This creature was absolutely gigantic. The other side of the room was many hundreds of feet away. Suddenly, it became clear in his mind, all of the features and details converged together into one shocking realization....

"THAT is the Dragon!" Bobill screamed in his subconscious.

It was true. Existing in reality right before his very eyes, Bobill beheld what was possibly the most dangerous living being in Skiddle Earth: The Serpenstiltzer Dragon, Domardacktilianofarjenseriumsan. With a deep, low, rumbling growl, Domard the Dragon continued his sniffing, knowing all too well that someone had encroached upon his domain. To Bobill's surprise, if he could be any more surprised, the Dragon spoke aloud, showing teeth that were easily twice the length of the Gabbin.

"Who *BE* thou?" asked Domard, in a horribly scratchy and booming voice.

He was still searching for the intruder. Bobill did not reply, for he was attempting to slowly and carefully pass around the Dragon and get to the exit door. Alas, poor Bobill's shoe grazed a coin on top of a stack, and it hit the floor with a faint 'click'. Domard's gaze snapped down to Bobill's exact position, and he asked again much louder,

"Who BE thou?!" Then he lowered his head closer. "There is no point in thy sneakment now. I hearest thine shuffling footwear, and I smellest thine pooting rear. Speak now! Or be turned to ashes."

Bobill stuttered a bit, but finally answered out of mindless fear. "I am Bobill Gabbin and I live in a mudhole!" he yelled.

Smoke rolled from Domard's nostrils, he looked irritated that he could not see Bobill.

"Gabbin, say thou?" asked Domard. "I should guess that thou hast come unto this place for a helping of my gold, correct?"

Bobill shook his head, then remembered that he was invisible, so he replied, "Certainly not... Mister Dragon sir. I was merely trying to locate my... invisible pants. Oh, here they are! Right on my invisible legs. I'll be taking my leave then! Good day!"

Bobill tried to run, but Domard shifted and dropped his other claw right in front of him, hearing his gold-kicking shoes.

"LIES!!" roared Domard. "I sawest thou enter, I gazed

upon thine shining wig, and I *peered* at the pilfering of one of the finest pieces of my hoard. The EarthStar, meteor of super-gold. Thou shalt not leave this place without first being not alive!"

The Dragon raised up and thrashed around, throwing all manner of sparkly objects and valuable goodies throughout the room. Bobill spun on his toe and sprinted to the far opposite wall; maybe he could somehow get out the front entrance. He got nearly halfway across the room before Domard's tail slapped down, blocking his way in that direction as well.

"This be MY gold and none others!" Domard screamed, as he clawed and snapped at the area he thought Bobill was in.

"I didn't see your name on it!" cried Bobill, having no idea what drove him to say such a thing.

"Did thou not?!" answered Domard in anger. "How doest *THIS* grab thee?!"

The Dragon rose up higher and quickly slashed his razor-sharp claws into a large flat section of wall.

'Domard's Tresure!' read the wall scratchings.

"Doest thou see it NOW?!" he said, seemingly pleased with himself.

"Yes, yes I do," squeaked Bobill. "However..." he trailed off.

"What say thee? Speak!"

Bobill paused a moment, then quickly replied, "You spelled 'treasure' wrong!"

He immediately ran toward Domard's tail, jumped at the least thick section, and slid over it, crashing flat to the floor on his back. Domard roared in explosive fury at the insulting quip and let loose his flaming vengeance. Waves of fire passed right over Bobill, singeing his nose hairs. Only Domard's own tail blocked the flames from vaporizing him. Just as Bobill got to his feet, the Dragon smashed him into the floor with the tail, dragging it over him, then whipped it back, tossing him through the air. Bobill flipped end over end until he landed, of all places, right on Domard's forehead.

Domard threw back his head and blew more flames all around, heating the room to three hundred twenty-one Kelvin. Bobill grabbed hold of Domard's eyelids and held tight, sweating intensely as the Dragon flailed violently. Then, the unthinkable happened. Domard blinked his eyes, and Bobill's ring was pulled from his finger. He watched in utter, sickening horror as it tumbled through the air, landed almost soundless amid the Dragon's wails of wrath, and sank into some unknown pile in the tremendously immeasurable hoard of gold. Bobill's grip failed him, and he was cast to the floor again in front of Domard.

"Well, well," said the Dragon. "Thou can be seen once more. But now *thee* will see... the inside of me."

Bobill knew he was done for. He grabbed the hilt of Stink in final desperation and prepared to charge. Maybe he could do it, if he defeated this monster, he would go down in history. He thought of returning to his home-town of Hometown, not only as its beloved mayor but now with a much more stunning title...

"Dragonslayer Bill," he whispered to himself. "Man, that would sound great."

He unsheathed his sword and ran at Domard, screaming like a maniac. Domard opened his jaws and rushed at Bobill, ready to bite down. Right as they were about to clash, Bobill slipped on a coin and fell flat on his back again. Domard snapped his jaws closed, shocked to not feel Gabbin flesh between his teeth. While this was going on, the coin that Bobill had slipped upon shot straight up in the air. All the way to the ceiling it went, glancing off a large stalactite. A crack tore through the base of the hanging stone, and it fell. Bobill rolled sideways to get out from under the Dragon just as the giant rock smashed into Domard's head.

The stalactite broke into many pieces, and Domard slumped down, his whole body going limp. Bobill stood and caught his breath. Then he went over to the Dragon's seemingly lifeless body and began to poke at it. There was no response. The Dragon was certainly possibly dead. For a time, Bobill searched the room looking for his ring, but it was in vain. No trace of it could be found, if he even knew what a trace of a ring would look like. He thought he was going to be sick. That little circle had come to be very useful, and he would've traded anything to have it back now. Feeling defeated, yet at least uneaten, he turned away from the treasure room and walked back up the long hall to the secret entrance.

When Bobill emerged from the door, he saw the Dorks were currently in the midst of holding a funeral for him. They threw down the flowers and kicked the makeshift casket off the mountain upon seeing his return, shouting and greeting him with joy. Bobill told them about his encounter with Domard, and of the Dragon's demise at the hands of a rock. The Dorks listened in wonder with mouths agape and eyes glistening, quite unable to believe all that had taken place.

After that, they all hurried inside, except Bobill who was very much enjoying being back out in the sun and breeze on the mountainside. He did eventually rise from his resting spot and traveled back down to join them. As they all stood in the hall of the treasure hoard, Forky got a bit emotional. He hadn't seen the inside of this place in a very long time; not since the fall of his people, when the Dragon first came and claimed the life of his grandfather, the Dork-Lord Fjörkensunn.

"My father, Florkus, led the survivors away and into a life of seemingly endless wandering after the fall of my grandfather," said Forky, turning to Bobill, who was the only one unaware of these new revelations. "We were living in tents and always looking for a new cave for sale. But none were on the market in those days, and we no longer had gold with which to purchase one even if there was. It was during those dark, miserable years, that I tried my hand at farming, and earned my... unfortunate title."

Bobill felt for the Dorks a bit now and tried to put some of their previous, outrageously foolish behavior out of his mind.

"I thought this was just a cave you stored gold in though," said Bobill. "Where did you live exactly?"

Forky turned back again to the far wall where the huge doors stood that Bobill assumed was just the front entrance. The Dork walked toward them, and the rest followed. He set his palms against the doors and heaved. With loud creaks and bangs, they swung open, revealing far more interior than Bobill could've imagined.

Forky then said to him, "Witness now, young Mister Gabbin... Solitudious, the hallowed city of the Dork-Lords."

Pathways, arches, pillars, bridges, doors, and entire buildings were spread out as far as the eye could see. It was much lighter here, for above were cut small holes to let light in from the outside of the mountain. Bobill went in with the Dorks and they walked down the ancient roads, taking in the majestic sights and craftwork of the Dorks of old. While they explored for a short time, the Dorks reminisced of the elder days when the halls were full of life and goodliness. Jerky told of how he used to smack mailboxes with an axe handle as a Dork-Lad, showing the dents that were still displayed upon them. Porky of course talked of all his favorite restaurants, and Corky showed Bobill the beard-barber shop he worked in as an apprentice for his first job.

"Shame Dorky couldn't be here to witness this with us," said Forky. "I know you think we didn't pay much heed to his passing, but it is the custom of the Dorks to act like we don't care, and then care a while later. I don't expect you to understand."

Bobill nodded to him, pretending like it made some sense.

Then Forky spoke up once more, addressing them all. "It is great to be back here, but we have much work to do yet. We have a Dragon's body to dispose of, and a Gabbin to pay! I'm sure he'll be eager to get home to his mud-hole soon."

"*That* I certainly am," replied Bobill.

"First, we'll carry out a portion of the treasure for you to take," said Forky. "Then, you can go as you wish, or stay and help us slice up this lizard. The choice is yours, and I wouldn't fault you for leaving if you have any idea of what a Dragon smells like inside."

"I suppose we'll see," said Bobill.

So, trip after trip they all made, carrying the proposed share of the riches of the mountain owed to Bobill out the front entrance. They heaped it in a pile on the side of the main road just outside. The problem now, was that there was too much treasure to carry. They sat down on the sharp rocks for a while trying to think of a way to get all the treasure to Bobill's home. Just then, they heard a noise coming from afar.

'SWOOSH!'

The wind blew, and there before them hovered Randolf in his new flying machine.

"How in the world did you escape the pit of doom that you fell into!?" asked Bobill.

Randolf smirked and replied, "Well you see, I decided

to build this here flying machine out of rocks and water that I managed to yank out of the walls on my way down. So, after falling four hundred and ninety-nine miles, this machine was finally complete. It took me a while, but it saved me in the long run. I nearly hit the bottom as the machine launched upward, and I caught a glimpse of a very unpillowed floor. So it's a good thing I'm such a crafty old Wiz!" Randolf smiled from ear to ear with great pride.

Suddenly, the machine exploded into a billion pieces. Randolf's smile flipped over. Forky surprisingly explained how the brave Bobill fought and defeated the Dragon all by himself, and they had taken back their Dork-Hall.

"Now Mister Gabbin just needs a way to carry his share back to his home," said Forky. "We had originally planned to come back with Bobill to Hometown, and maybe find or have a place built there for ourselves. We've certainly got the money for it now. We did not know if we would be able to actually defeat the Dragon. Although that was the plan, it was fairly insane, so we mostly figured we'd just sneak in and steal a bunch of our gold back and leave. But now that we see our home of old is still intact and undestroyed by the Dragon, I believe we will be staying here, and attempting to restore it back to the way it was before the reeking creature stole it away."

Randolf replied, "Good, a true Dork-Lord there shall be

once more upon the throne of Solitudious then. I shall make sure that our Gabbin gets back home safe with his spoils. Take care and farewell for now, my Dork acquaintances."

He then shook each of the Dorks' hands, all except Porky, for Randolf had seen him recently picking his nose. Then the Wizard snapped his fingers and smacked his staff on a dead branch. The branch ever so slowly turned into a huge wagon for Bobill to pull. They began loading it with priceless items until the wheels buckled. Forky stepped up to Bobill once more.

"Farewell—and thank you for all you've done for us, Bobill, we shall never forget it," he said.

All the Dorks bowed low, and said together in a quite expected, yet still frightful voice, "We are ever at your servings, Bobill!"

Randolf jumped on to Bobill's shoulders and smacked him on the head until he pulled the thousand-ton cart to a decent speed. Then the two started off on the long journey back toward Hometown.

As the waving Dorks began to fade into the distance behind them, Bobill could hear Forky cry out, "Now let's chop up that fat flying lizard."

Chapter 13:
Going Home... NOT!

After Bobill had pulled his treasure cart for an hour, he needed to stop and rest. Randolf jumped down from his shoulders and began doing stretches on the side of the road. So far, they had made it about twelve hundred feet; not quite even reaching the town of FakeTown yet.

"We've got to figure out a better way to do this, Rand," said Bobill, still panting.

"Oh, good grief," replied Randolf. "Always with the complaints. I shall see if I can go find a rat or a gopher with which to turn into something large and useful. Wait here and get some air in those chubby lungs."

With that, Randolf dove into some nearby bushes and vanished. A few moments later, Bobill nearly fell to the ground when an earth-shaking rumble struck. It was no natural occurrence. He grabbed the cart to steady himself as he looked back to the mountain. Massive amounts of rock were raining down one side, as if an explosion had taken place there.

Then Bobill saw it. Turning sharply around the curve of the mountain's middle heights, was a winged nightmare in flight. The Dragon was very much alive. Bobill began freaking out. He searched and called for Randolf, but the Wizard was nowhere to be found. The Gabbin would have to go alone. He had to do something to make sure the Dorks weren't killed, and that FakeTown stayed safe as well. Who knows what that sky-serpent would do in his vengeful fury? So off he ran, leaving his cart behind and heading back to the mountain.

Just as Bobill reached the front gate of Solitudious, the Dorks were running out in a panic.

"What happened?!" cried Bobill.

Forky slid to a stop in front of him replying, "Didn't we say bye to you already?! Anyway, just as my first axe-stroke fell upon the beast's neck, it awoke from its death-like slumber. It dodged the axe and attacked us. We barely got out of the treasure room alive. We then barred the doors, but it evidently broke out of the back side someh—HECK!!"

A terrified Forky pointed behind Bobill, but before he could react, Domard swooped overhead, unleashing flames upon them. They all jumped and rolled out of the way just in time as the ground and surrounding shrubs went up in a raging fire. The blaze spread quickly, blocking the way back into the mountain. The Dragon circled around for another attack. Slerky drew his bow and fired three times at Domard as he approached, but the arrows shattered upon his scaly hide. Jerky had thrown his axe as well, which also had no effect. It simply glanced off Domard's face and tumbled back down to stick in the dirt.

"Run!" yelled Forky.

They all took off toward FakeTown as the Dragon blasted the area just behind them with more fire.

"Where is Randolf?" asked Corky as he sprinted beside Bobill.

"Gone," replied Bobill. "He ran into the bushes looking for something more suitable to pull my treasure wagon."

Forky grunted in irritation saying, "Always when we're in the most trouble is when that looney old geezer decides to disappear!"

The group continued dodging fireballs and snapping jaws all the way to FakeTown.

Bobill and the Dorks passed the treasure cart and called out for Randolf as they proceeded with their running. Again, the Wizard was nowhere to be seen. FakeTown came into view and Bobill cried for joy when he saw a man standing on the roof of a house with a cannon at the ready. The Dragon was still swooping and breathing fire at the group. Thankfully, his aim was terrible due to his eyes still adjusting to the light outside of the treasure room he had spent so much time in. The group got closer still to the town, and the cannon man on the rooftop prepared to fire at the Dragon. Bobill plugged his ears and smiled, feeling hopeful that the Dragon's tough exterior could not withstand such a weapon. He smiled wider, tensing up and waiting for the 'boom' of the cannon. The man was still in the lighting position. What was he waiting for? The group began shouting at the fool.

"Do it now!" they all repeatedly cried, but the man stood firm and unmoving.

"Crap darn it!!" screamed Forky. "It's a daggone friggin' cardboard cutout!"

Bobill's smirk was obliterated, but he had a thought.

"We can't bring him closer to the town," he said. "Let's go wide around it and take this air lizard to the river!"

They bounded off, rounding far to the left of FakeTown and finally coming to the banks of the Solitary River. Domard swept over them again, his vision improving. He unleashed now a more powerful attack: a swirling cone of flames wreathed in ice and lightning. It closed in quickly on the group, and just before it consumed their toes, they jumped all at once, landing in the waters of the river. The huge wall of electric ice-fire passed over the surface of the water only moments after they'd sunk below it. Bobill came up a minute later coughing and splashing amongst chunks of burnt ice; he sucked at swimming and needed to get back to the bank.

He was yanked forward and quickly pulled to land by Slerky, who had worked as a swimming instructor in his youth. Though he had never worked with water, only mounds of gold coins. Bobill stood to his feet, took note that all the Dorks were back on land and accounted for, and looked to the west. The Dragon was crossing the setting sun on the far side of the river, turning toward them again for another fiery assault.

"Give me your socks, NOW!" cried Bobill suddenly.

The Dorks looked like they thought he had lost his mind.

"Get 'em off!!" he yelled again, slapping at them this time.

They obeyed now, as he took off his own. Then, with his quick and fat little Gabbin hands, he tied all the socks together. The Dorks were confused as ever, but Bobill had a look of determination in his eyes that they could not help but notice. The Gabbin quickly scanned the area and found two perfect trees standing side by side near the water's edge. He ran over to the trees, and the Dorks saw the Dragon dive low over the river straight at them. Bobill tied the long sock chain's ends to each tree and began to pull the center back.

"Help me!" cried Bobill, and the Dorks ran to him.

They had no idea what he was trying to do, but they grabbed hold of the stretchy chain of socks along with him and pulled it back as far as they possibly could.

"You intend to fire a projectile at him with this?" said Forky, understanding now.

Bobill nodded, then a sickly feeling fast overcame him, and his hope was lost. They had nothing to place in the sock chain to shoot. Domard was upon them now, and his most powerful blast was charging; only seconds away from wiping the group from the face of Skiddle Earth. But Bobill remembered something, he hastily unzipped his fanny pack and pulled forth from it the meteor of supergold. Forky's eyes went wide in amazement.

"That... is the EarthStar of Fjörkensunn... the utmost prized possession of the Dork-Lords!" said Forky. "You cannot..." the Dork's voice trailed off, knowing it was their only chance.

He nodded to Bobill, and the little Gabbin placed the

shining golden rock in the center of their makeshift slingshot.

"ONE-TWO-THREE!!" Bobill shouted as fast as he could.

He and the Dorks all released their grasp simultaneously, and the EarthStar sailed at blinding speed toward the Dragon. Domard's final blast was releasing at that very moment, but not much came forth. The meteor of supergold passed straight through the flame, ice, and lightning, then into the Dragon's mouth, lodging firmly within his lengthy throat. Domard tried to gasp for air but could not. His wings and tail seized up, and his eyes turned into large X's. With a tremendous crash, the mighty Dragon fell into the river, erupting massive amounts of water high in the air. Bobill and the Dorks ran back down to the water's edge and looked on as the slippery, wet, lifeless body of the Dragon bobbed and rolled over in the river's current, disappearing in the distance. The body continued on until it reached the falls at Bread Ridges and plummeted into the dark abyss.

Several seconds after the Dragon was vanquished, Randolf came speedwalking up out of the weeds.

"Snuck off for some fishing while the Wizard does all the work to find a decent steed, eh?" asked Randolf with one eyebrow high.

Bobill started to explain what happened, but Randolf cut him off abruptly.

"Now, now, Mister Gabbin, I can easily assume what has taken place here by all of the fire.... You were trying to cook again, weren't you?"

Forky stepped in, loudly clearing his throat, and began to correct Randolf. But Randolf cut him off too.

"That's quite enough," said the Wizard. "It doesn't matter who did it now, just know that you are all equally to blame. Let us get back to the wagon and stop fooling around—Mister Gabbin has a long journey ahead of him."

So off they went, returning once more to FakeTown.

"We need to stop here for a moment," said Forky. "There is some business we must attend to."

They went up the stairs and across the town porch, passing all of the various cardboard folk standing about. Randolf was puzzled by all that he saw, for he had not come through this town before. He did not, however, question the rest of the group about it since he was eager to leave and didn't want to listen to a long, boring story that he wasn't in. The group strode directly down the main road, coming to the town hall at the end and entering inside, then took the hidden passage into the secret basement.

THE GABBIN

As they passed into the main chamber, Gourden, his daughter Clumbette, and several others stepped out of the darkness to greet them.

"The Dragon is no more," said Forky with a half-grin. "He is drowned in the river and will never threaten your town again. You are welcome now to come and help yourselves to however much... I mean a *bit* of the mountain's riches."

Gourden and Forky then engaged in a firm handshake like ones only told about in ancient legends. Randolf, Bobill and the Dorks exited the town hall, followed now by the newly free people of FakeTown, many of whom had never seen the outside. They spread out across the porch, taking in the sights of this new world.

Clumbette looked up at the clear sky in awe, and squinting in the light she said, "So that is the sun. A thing I've only ever dreamt of...."

Corky leaned in and stuttered, "Umm, actually that's the moon. It's nighttime. I wouldn't try looking at the sun like that when it comes up tomorrow, it'll burn your eyeballs."

She then gave him a look of bewilderment and wonder. Randolf and Bobill decided to stay in the town that night with the Dorks and get started again in the morning.

Going Home... NOT!

Bobill awoke to the sound of screaming. It was the townfolk, overwhelmed by the sight of the sun rising over the Mountain of Solitude.

Later, everyone had a breakfast of fish from the river, and whatever else they could hunt or find. All was cooked by Porky in his pot hat. He had mostly forgiven the folk of the town at this point and was glad to be making food rather than being food. Not that there was evidence of the FakeTowners doing such things mind you. Randolf and Forky promised to send out for supply wagons as soon as possible and begin a new trade route for the town and mountain. With all of the endless gold in the halls of the Dorks, the place would thrive better than it was ever intended to. Forky spoke with Gourden a while, working out some more deals together, and after, the Dork came to Bobill with news.

"Some things have changed, Mister Gabbin," he said. "We will be joining along to see that you make it home safe with your share of gold. Gourden will keep the treasure hoard safe here and even offered to repair the side of the mountain that the Dragon destroyed while we're gone."

Bobill was happy and sad at the same time. Happy because the Dorks would now be accompanying him on the return journey, but sad due to the fact that he would be traveling home with the Dorks. He and the Dorks said their goodbyes to the people of FakeTown and departed once more to the river. Randolf had already gone ahead and brought the wagon from its abandoned position; it was waiting for them near the boat that Bobill and the Dorks had built to cross the river.

They were wondering how Randolf had moved the incredibly heavy load by himself. When Bobill and the Dorks arrived at the river, they found Randolf standing proudly by the wagon. Tied to the front of it were about four hundred snakes of various size and color, all under Randolf's command. The smiling Wizard snapped his fingers and the snakes slid forward, driving the cart on to the boat. The group all boarded the vessel, took their respective positions, and sailed back across the Solitary River.

Chapter 14:
For Real This Time

After the wagon filled with treasure was offloaded from the boat, everyone piled on to the seats that stuck out here and there from it. All except Bobill that is. The Gabbin disliked anything serpentious in nature and dared not approach the wagon. In fact, he had stayed well away from it on the entire river voyage, though the snakes did not move from their spot whatsoever. Randolf told him to stop being a baby and climb on, for his stubby gams would slow them down if he walked the whole way. Bobill folded his arms, closed his eyes, and turned his head away from them. Then he stamped one foot hard on the ground in protest.

Jerky quickly tossed a lasso at the rebellious Gabbin, which tightened around his legs and dropped him to the ground. The wagon rolled on again and the Dorks ironically held their ears as Bobill whined for several dozen miles. Randolf finally had enough, he zapped the four hundred snakes, and they turned into five horses with snakeskin and flicky tongues.

"Is that more to your liking, your *majesty*?!" yelled Randolf sarcastically.

Bobill nodded furiously, so Corky went back and untied him. The Gabbin pulled himself onto the cart, seating his backside in the front next to Randolf. All the while he was trying hard not to puke at the sight of the freaky horses. They passed unhindered through timber moose country, aside from Randolf having to blast apart the giant fallen tree across their path for the wagon to proceed. A tree that some of them remembered well. Bobill shuddered when he thought of the cave that lie somewhere in this general location and wondered if the demon that dwelled within watched them even now. But he dismissed the thought, for Randolf was with him this time.

Soon they were far out of the area and approaching Bread Ridges once more. Thankfully, new rope bridges had been built since they had come this way originally. A new guard stood watch now in a little shack just before the first bridge; he was far less mean-looking than the previous one. Randolf steered the wagon over to the man, muttering a few greetings. The guard stepped out and inspected the wagon, obviously disturbed by the snake-horses.

"Your toll today is $18.32," said the guard. "Just so you

know, the bridge restoration fund was recently increased to fifty cents after some reckless maniacs tore up a bunch of the old bridges."

Randolf pulled his Wizard-wallet from his kilt and found that he had less than he thought; for inside the wallet was only a single $17 bill. The Wizard looked at the Dorks and Bobill, but they told him they'd eaten their cash days ago. The guard shook his head and went back to his shack to fetch his bashing club. The group went into a panic trying to figure out some way to pay the toll. Just as the guard came back, Porky found a few dollars wedged between his right-side, upper back teeth. The money was handed over, and the guard gave back the appropriate change. Right when Randolf started to pull away however, the guard raised his hand.

"Hold up there, pops," said the guard, much to Randolf's annoyance.

Randolf turned to him again, eyebrows high in expectation.

"You paid for the group of travelers, but this here cart is another charge entirely. Pull it over on the scale to the side of the shack."

So Randolf backed up the wagon, then swung to the right, driving up onto a large, square platform. A nearby mechanism on a pole displayed numbers with flipping panels to show the price. It stopped at $9,001.47. There was no other choice now. Randolf whipped the reins and circled the wagon hard, accelerating rapidly as it came around to face the bridge again. The guard shouted and ran after them, swinging his club angrily. The snake-horses shattered the crossing gates as the wagon dropped sharply onto the first rope bridge, causing it to sag dangerously low. Creaking and popping noises were heard in the planks and ropes around them.

The guard slid to a halt at the broken gate and pulled out his radio to call in backup to cut them off at the other side. The only problem being that radios didn't exist, and the guard was just shouting into a rock, so no one heard his calls for help. Randolf continued whipping the steeds and they sped across the bridges of Bread Ridges, successfully reaching the other side by the next morning. Now they had to travel all the way back through Kirkwoods.

A few days had passed, and the group still rode on through Kirkwoods. Almost nothing of interest had happened so far, aside from Randolf falling asleep and tumbling off the cart, then having to run two miles to catch back up when he awoke. Eventually, they did run into some trouble. There was a sudden jolt as one of the wagon's wheels struck an exceptionally aggressive tree root. The wagon slid to a dragging halt and leaned to the back left corner. The wheel was a mangled wreck and would need repairing. Randolf said that he couldn't use his staff powers to fix the wheel, for he needed to conserve its energy for using as a light, as he had been doing since crossing into the woods.

Slerky, Porky and Forky were still fast asleep strapped into their wagon seats. The rest of them spread out to look for some fixinwood. Bobill followed the path in the direction from whence they had just come, and not far down it he found the root of their problems: the tree root. It was all knotty and disrespectful looking. Bobill kicked it and immediately wished he hadn't, for of wood it was made, and no soft sort at that. He flopped on his bum in the middle of the dark road to complain, and there before him he spied a golden cup. It had obviously fallen off the wagon when it collided with the root. Bobill slid himself forward and grabbed it up. He studied it all around, admiring the craftsmanship and sparkling jewels that were set in a row and encircling the cup just beneath its rim. On one of its lower sides was a faint inscription; Bobill struggled in the dimness to read it.

'Dishwasher Safe', it read.

Bobill knew not what it meant.

In a sudden, random fit of foolery, Bobill lifted the golden cup high, and proclaimed in a deep pompous tone,

"Bow ye down now to King Bobe! Lord of all Dorks!"

With that, he stuck his lips out impressively far, and pretended to drink from the cup. He expected for there to be nothing more than air inside, but he was dead wrong. Something slipped between his lips, rolled down his tongue, and wedged itself tight into his throat. He began flailing and coughing, then pounding his chest. When that didn't work, he began punching himself in the throat repeatedly to no avail. He found that he *could* breathe somewhat; there seemed to be a hole in the center of whatever was stuck in there.

He tried calling for help, but it just sounded like a wheezing goose, and was not very loud. He had to get back to the wagon, but before he could stand up, something slapped him hard on the back. The object flew out of his throat, landing silently in his hand. He didn't look at it however, but instead turned his head around to see who or what had struck him. It was no welcoming sight.

There in the shadows behind him, stood Gorizzle the Fiddler. The monkey was creepy as ever. He walked slowly around Bobill to stand in front of him, then yanked Bobill to his feet sooner than he could react. Bobill was about to sprint away, but Gorizzle just stood still and grinned at him. So instead, the Gabbin took a couple of cautionary backward steps, his eyes ever trained on the treacherous primate. He gripped the hilt of Stink, but something happened then that he could've never imagined.

Gorizzle bowed low, right arm across his monkey-chest, and said, "It is good to see that you are well. Know that I am well as well, and that I am ever at your servings!"

He stood up straight, and Bobill saw now that something was *off* about Gorizzle. Like it wasn't the monkey at all, but some imposter wearing a suit, or even his very skin.

"BOBILL!!" screamed a voice in the distance just then.

He glanced behind, but none of his companions were near enough to see. That's all the time it took, for when he turned back, Gorizzle had vanished into blackness, never to be seen again. Bobill could've sworn he heard a fiddle playing softly far off in the deep woods, growing ever fainter until it was no more.

He picked up his golden cup from the ground, then remembered the unknown item still clasped in his other hand. He opened the hand close to his nose, and there he beheld an unbelievable sight. It was his ring. Somehow, against all mathematical standards of probability, it had ended up in his own wagon. He thought he would not lay eyes on it again for the rest of his days. He glanced around suspiciously, then shoved the gracious little thing into his fanny pack, double zipping it tightly. When he got back to the wagon, everyone was sitting on top waiting for him, and the wheel was good as new.

"Corky tried to tie some fixinwood to the wheel and made it worse," said Randolf. "So I said 'heck on it' and ended up just zapping the darn thing with my staff. I suppose you'll have to get over it if we run out of light and/or get attacked."

Bobill merrily flung himself back into his seat and was so glad of his good fortunes that he did not tell them of anything that had taken place. He tossed the golden cup into the mound of treasure behind him, and they rode onward.

At one point, the path ahead split. They hadn't noticed this when they came through from the other direction.

"Ahh," said Randolf. "This route can bring us out of the woods a little sooner and make for some different scenery for the rest of the trip. It will take us to the same destination, and we won't have to pass through Neebo's land again. I think he's seen enough of us for one lifetime."

Everyone else kind of shrugged carelessly, so Randolf steered the wagon south onto the new path. The Dorks then pulled out their trumpets that Bobill thought and hoped they had lost. They began to play them and loudly sing:

"We crossed the lands and defeated the Dragon,
we did it ourselves with some help from a Gabbin!
Nearly eaten by dinos and Trolls,
an Elf and an Ape served us buttercake rolls!
Through forest green and over bridges brown,
we sailed 'cross a river and came to a town!
Past fake people and under the floor,
then climbed up a mountain to find the secret door!
The gold was claimed,
and the Dragon gave chase,
he tried to burn us,
but we shot him in the face!
He fell that day and he was no more,
he drowned in the river that was mentioned before!
Now back we ride with a Gabbin so round,
Randolf's driving him to his Hometown!
Through the valleys and over the mountains,
we sing this song and drink from the fountains!
With cheese in the dirt,
and dirt in our hair,
and hair on our toes,
we goes, and goes, and GOES!"

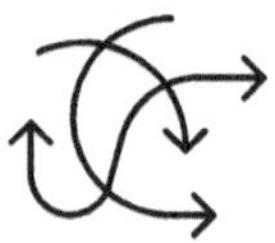

Chapter 15:
Lost Once More

The rising sun shone brightly on Bobill's little round face as his gold-laden wagon came at last to the southern exit of Kirkwoods. He had been dead asleep ever since the Dorks finally got tired of singing. He sat up and wiped the drool from his mouth and shirt, blinking vigorously in the long-awaited sunlight and fairly surprised to see Forky next to him driving. Randolf was on one of the side seats behind them conked out. Bobill rubbed his eyes and could see now the path in front of them. The road looked to run up into a range of mountains.

Bobill piped up. "Where are we?"

Forky looked over to him with eyebrows high. "We are coming now to the far eastern reaches of the Mimson Mountains. A winding path cuts through them here." He motioned ahead with an elbow.

Up and up they went, the air growing ever cooler. Snow eventually began to fall, and the snake-horses struggled to pull the weighty cart up the steep path that was quickly piling high with snowdrifts. Many hours passed, and they had now come to the highest point of their road: a wide, flat passage that curved around the high peak of Mount Snowfius. Bobill leaned back and gazed over Forky, in total awe at the sight of the white, glistening, twisted pinnacle of the Mimson Mountains. Though he soon forgot all about the view when he realized how cold he was. He reached in the back of the wagon and pulled out a large, golden pot with a lid, then placed it in his seat and wedged himself down inside.

Once he was crammed in, he pulled the lid on tight. It really didn't help much aside from blocking the merciless wind. Forky kept the wagon moving as Porky and Corky tried to foolishly light a fire on one of the back seats to keep warm and possibly cook something. The snowfall was turning into a blizzard, and the sun faded away. Forky strained to see in the blinding storm, and carefully guided the snake-horses around the left side of a snowy hill.

Without warning, the hill exploded and a huge beast came forth at the wagon. It was a Snow Troll, apparently attracted by the chicken that Porky had somehow obtained and was now roasting on a spit over the backseat fire. The snake-horses panicked and hurled themselves forward, nearly throwing everyone off the wagon. Randolf woke up just in time to grab his seat as he was sliding off. He climbed back on and held tight in confusion.

THE GABBIN

Jerky climbed over the mound of gold from the other side of the cart and yelled to him, "Snow Troll!"

The monstrous, furry, white thing was in a full run, easily gaining on the wagon. Slerky fired arrows, but the Troll swatted them away like long, pointy flies. Corky yanked the roasting chicken from the spit and launched it at the beast's face. The Troll snatched it up fast and swallowed it whole, still running. Randolf jumped to the back, switching places with Porky and Corky. The Wizard mumbled some magical words and held his staff high. Lightning came down from the heavens, striking within inches of the pursuing monster.

Randolf mumbled again, raising the staff higher now. Piercing bright bolts of yellow electricity came down in several bursts, blasting all around the Troll. At last, the final strike made a connection. The Snow Troll was zapped right between his fat hairy shoulder blades, causing it to tumble forward, then end over end, gathering snow as it flipped. A few moments later and the Troll was completely encased in a massive, rolling snowball that threatened to crush the wagon and its passengers flat. It was at this time that Forky saw the path narrowing and sharply turn off to the left, but they were traveling much too fast to follow it.

"Hold on!!" cried Forky as the wagon suddenly dropped down the incredibly steep mountainside.

Lost Once More

The snowball came immediately after, still growing ever larger. Forky wrestled the snake-horses with the reigns, trying desperately to keep the wagon straight as it whipped side to side, occasionally tipping up on two wheels. After a good while of this, and miraculously missing all the trees, boulders, and chasms, the slope began to level out. Forky regained control and swerved hard to the right. Then, the fifty-foot snowball passed them by, disappearing in the distance. Before Forky could catch his breath, Randolf had tossed him into the gold pile and had retaken his place in the driver's seat.

Bobill peeked his head out of his golden pot, looked wide-eyed at Randolf, and asked, "What happened?"

The travelers continued down the rest of the mountain, escaping the wrathful blizzard. Back they had come to dry, grassy plains and soon found their path once more. They had made good time through the mountain pass, and not long after the sun set, they came to a little grouping of houses and stores. It was a welcoming sight of civilization that had not been witnessed by their travel-weary eyes in many a day.

"This is the village of Debris," said Randolf. "I know folk here who may be able to set us up somewhere comfortable for the night."

Randolf pulled the wagon in behind a large building, doing his best to conceal it, and motioned for the rest of them to follow him inside. Bobill and the Dorks trailed behind him, walking in through the front door under a big sign that read,

'The Motel of the Glancing Goaty'.

The name made little to no sense, but none of them cared at all. The innkeeper greeted them warmly and seemed glad to see Randolf. Perhaps he wasn't just making things up and actually did know this person.

"This is my old friend, Percival Picklepants," said Randolf, gesturing to the tubby, balding man before them. "I have stayed at this very motel many a time over the years since they offer a senior discount and got to know the fellow well. He doesn't get out much anymore due to his business and his fun-hating wife, Plentilda."

Percival laughed and told them, "Right you are. Though Plenti's not all that bad, just likes to run a tight chip around here."

Bobill crossed his eyes and frowned. "A tight what?" he asked impolitely.

Percival just looked at him a moment, scratching his wide, wiry beard, then he replied, "Well anyhow, what do you say you fellows tell me of your travels, and if it's fairly intrestin', I'll put you up tonight for free."

They all sat down in the main hall on some cushiony seats in front of a roaring fire and told the innkeeper of their marvelous journey. He was bored to tears and had already heard at least three better stories that day, so they had to pay for their room.

The next morning found the group of travelers well rested and ready to set out once more. But not till after they'd eaten their fill of breakfast and said their goodbyes to the innkeeper and his rude wife. The group took their leave of the motel and as they rounded the corner to the cart, they saw twenty or thirty people running away from it with armloads of gold.

"Thieves!" cried Bobill, throwing a rock in a particular direction.

But it was too late, the hoodlums of Debris had made off with a fair amount, though admittedly the large pile of treasure didn't seem to have even a dent made in it.

"Such is the way of things," said Randolf. "Good thing I cursed the treasure so that anyone who takes it will suffer from crippling flatulence and everything they eat for the next six years will taste like the wrong end of a cowpie."

Bobill snapped his attention to Randolf and began to look sickly.

"Calm yourself, Mister Gabbin, all of us here are excluded from the curse. I did so because the gold is obviously yours, and since the rest of us are helping to guard it, I didn't want the curse to transfer to one of us for simply retrieving a fallen item from the cart."

Bobill sighed in relief and pulled himself onto the front passenger seat.

"Let's get out of here before this whole town starts smelling like fartballs," said Jerky.

The rest hopped on, and they rode away out the western gates of Debris.

The group moved on through the lands of Vim Valley at a good pace, not stopping for any reason. They ate on the move, dropped deuces from the back of the wagon, and ran over hitchhikers like there was no tomorrow.

By the next morning, they arrived at the borders of the Zungle Jungle. It wasn't anywhere near the size of Kirkwoods and was not known to have many threats within.

So aside from a few strange noises and the occasional darting small animal, they had no trouble there at all. Except that's only what they thought. A smelly creature climbed through the dense foliage above, ever following, glaring, and creeping. It was an angry thing indeed, for a certain Gabbin named Bobill down below possessed an item it desired greatly; something that wasn't shaped like a square or a triangle whatsoever. This creature was waiting for his chance to strike. As soon as the group rested, he would clobber Bobill like the tubby thief he was and take back what was rightfully his.

Later that night, it grew a bit too dark for Randolf to continue driving. He was tired, trusted no one else's skills, and he had forgotten to charge his staff back at the motel. The wagon was halted, and the group set up a small campsite on the side of the path. Corky lit a fire, while Porky scraped some things together for dinner. There was a small amount of chicken and ham left, but Porky really wanted a side dish to go with it. He quickly set eyes on clusters of delicious-looking fruits hanging high in a jungle tree.

"Slerky, lasso that there tree and pull it down so I can get my hands on some of those Züt-Fruits," said Porky, knowing their proper name.

Slerky tossed his lasso, getting purchase on the crown of the tree in a single attempt. Corky and Jerky helped him bend the forty-foot tree's top to the ground with a great effort, then Forky hammered down a huge stake in the ground that they could tie the rope to. This way they could gather all the fruit they wanted. The Züt-Fruits were cracked open and found to be quite ripe and juicy. The meat was cooked and the whole group sat around the fire eating and laughing into the night.

Randolf was the first to slip out of consciousness, followed by Corky and Porky. Half an hour later, Jerky and Slerky passed out as well. It was nearing midnight now, and Forky conversed with Bobill for a time still. The fire became nothing but faintly glowing coals as the two gave in to their nodding heads and drooping eyelids. They bid each other a good night and retired to their respective sleeping bags.

Not long ago, Bobill would have been frightened out of his mind at the nightly noises of the wild jungle, unable to so much as close his eyes. Now, after all he had experienced on this amazing journey, he heeded them not and fell fast asleep under the dark Züt-Fruit trees. If only the foolish Gabbin had known what lurked in the shadows above.

Out from the reeking depths of the Mimson Mountain Caverns it had crawled, and it would stop at nothing to exact vengeance on this helpless, sleeping fatty. The creature silently descended the branches, coming nearer to Bobill with stealthy caution. Bobill lay flat on his back, snoring away in a deep sleep without a care in the world. His neck was now within feet of the disgusting creature's boney, unwashed fingers, as they outstretched to throttle the poor, unsuspecting Gabbin.

Half a moment before the creature's hands grabbed hold, Bobill stirred in his sleep as he dreamt of heroically slaying various beasts of all different sorts. Without waking, Bobill reached down and unsheathed Stink in a flash, swiping the blade wildly around. The creature backed up on the low branch it still clung to in sheer terror, until it realized that Bobill was only dreaming. The evil grin returned to its face, and it waited patiently for Bobill's dream to take him somewhere less violent. The Gabbin's little knife slowed, but before it dropped back to the ground, Bobill swung it once more and let go.

The blade whistled through the air for a moment, then sliced straight through the rope tied between the stake in the ground and the tightly bent tree that the creature was clinging to. The tree instantly snapped upright, throwing the creature up and over the jungle canopy at blinding speed. The piercing screams of the stinky creature woke Bobill, but only long enough for him to grab his tiny sword and slip it safely back into its sheath. Bobill peacefully fell back to sleep with a smile of total ignorance upon his face.

At the crack of dawn, most of the group was up and preparing to leave, as well as kicking and yelling at those who weren't. After a quick bite to eat, they were on the wagon again. It took only a couple of hours before they passed out from under the trees of the Zungle Jungle and came to the shores of an absolutely enormous lake. It may as well have been the ocean, for no land could be seen across from where they stood.

"This is the big lake, 'PimWimQuim'," said Randolf, gazing out over the endless waters. "Our brave and tireless snake-horses have done all they can for us. We must turn them loose now and find another means to traverse this body of water. We have no choice but to cut straight across, for it is a three hundred fifty-seven-mile journey around either side."

Bobill rolled his eyes and Randolf jumped down, cutting the snake-horses free. The five strange beasts ran off, back into the jungle behind.

"I say we seal up the sides of the wagon nice and tight, make some oars, and row ourselves over this lake," said Forky.

Everyone thought the idea was completely ridiculous, but they did it anyway. All the necessary modifications were made, and the wagon was pushed into the water. The group rowed with all their might for hours, but they only traveled about four thousand inches. They were tired and took a short break. Just then, a cave-ish looking man came up to them in a boat of his own.

His name was Papa-San, and he offered to pull the wagon-boat across the lake. His cave-boat (as he called it) had some sort of mechanism on the back end that propelled it forward with great force. Papa-San explained how he had built it himself, and it would power the cave-boat for hours with only a few turns of a crank. None of them had seen anything like it before, except Randolf, who was likely lying. A rope was tied between the two boats, and the long voyage to the other side of PimWimQuim began. All any of them had to do was kick back and wait.

Two days of incredibly boring sailing had passed, and the boats came at last to the lake's exit point that flowed down between Some Mountains close to Bobill's town. The only problem was, someone had built a gate blocking access to Crim Creek, a super frigging large gate. Between the high peaks of the mountains on either side of the creek it stood, rising five thousand two hundred and eighty feet tall. Randolf told Papa-San they would figure it out and that he could go now if he wished. Bobill gave him some gold for his troubles, and they all thanked the caveman.

Eventually, the group formulated a plan to hurdle this great obstacle. They gathered all the ropes they had and tied them end to end. One end of the full length was tied to the front of the wagon-boat, and the other was carried with them as they scaled the lofty heights of the gate.

It was a physically impossible task, but they saw it through nonetheless. They dug their fingertips into the smooth surface of the gate wall and climbed. Halfway up, Randolf told them that he had business to attend to and would rejoin them shortly. He let go of the wall and fell. His kilt then flared out into a kind of parachute, and he steered away, vanishing off into the distance.

The rest of them shook their heads in disbelief at the Wizard's timing. The Dorks proceeded upward, now following Bobill to the top. The Gabbin reached it first, throwing the end of the rope over the far side of the gate. He stood on top waiting for them, and suddenly, he got an urge to put his ring on. Bobill quickly slipped it on and became unvisible. Then he hugged himself because of how special the ring made him feel.

Finally, as the Dorks neared the top, he pulled it back off his chubby finger. He held it aloft and leaned in to kiss it on the lips. Just then, Jerky came up over the edge and the sick sight of Bobill startled him. He stumbled backward, and to stop himself, he grabbed Bobill's arm. Jerky's hands slid down the arm to the Gabbin's hand, pulling the ring away from him. Bobill watched as Jerky fell off the gate with the ring. He kicked off his shoes and threw his wig aside, running to the edge to dive, but Forky grabbed his big toe with his pointer finger and thumb to stop him. Bobill slapped flat against the side of the gate, and Forky pulled him up.

"Wrong way, Bobill, your home is in *this* direction!" Forky said, motioning to the west with his elbow.

Bobill peered down as Jerky grabbed the rope and slid himself to a smoking halt, still three-quarters of the way up. Beyond that, Bobill's magical and wondrous piece of fingerwear disappeared into the deep, endless lake. He thought for a passing moment of cutting the rope and letting Jerky fall, but he knew that would be an evil deed. He was just very upset. After losing it before, it was finally all his, and almost back with him to the safety of his home. He had been imagining dancing and singing with the ring, eating and telling stories by the fire with the ring, and one day, he would've married that ring.... Wait, what?

Anyway, he cried now, for it was lost once more, most likely forever, and the Dorks awkwardly looked away, assuming he was just going crazy or didn't sleep well the previous night. Jerky climbed back up to the top and was filled with gladness to see that Bobill was so concerned for his wellbeing. Bobill dried his eyes, nodded in acceptance to the lake behind them, then turned now toward home. They passed a lone chair in the center of the thick gate wall. Sitting in the chair was a sign with the words 'Out to Lunch' scribbled hastily upon it.

They paid it no mind but crossed to the edge that overlooked Crim Creek. The rope was tied around Porky's waist, and he was shoved off the top of the gate. The wagon was yanked to the top, and Bobill and the other Dorks jumped on just as it plummeted down the other side into the creek below. Porky was able to climb the rope fast enough to get back on the wagon before it splashed into the water. It went in deep, nearly hitting the bottom, but shot back up to the surface and settled out, never losing a single piece of gold.

It calmly floated down Crim Creek, passing the ever-lowering mountains on either side until they smoothed out into rolling green fields and eventually, dense forest. They steered the wagon-boat to the shore near a crossing where a road lay before them that cut through the woods. Thankfully, the wagon-boat was also still a regular wagon and still had its wheels. It was tough going, but they managed to push it the last several miles until they came to a large sign that made Bobill smile from ear to chubby ear.

'Welcome to the town of Hometown!' the sign proclaimed.

They pressed on until they finally arrived at last to Bobill's own mudhole where Randolf awaited them at the front door. He claimed that he went ahead to make sure Bobill's house was ready and in order, but they quietly assumed he just didn't want to climb the rest of the gate. The Dorks and Randolf helped Bobill make his house better than ever, covering the old mud with brand new mud, and building a fortified, secret room for his gold and treasure. They spent a couple of weeks there, and Bobill didn't mind the company at all. They sang songs, reminisced of their journey, and ate oranges from an apple tree located within the town.

At last, one afternoon, the Dorks said they needed to be on their way, as they were growing eager to get back to their new Dorken kingdom. Many thanks were spoken, dozens of hands were shaken, and promises of future gatherings were made. The Dorks then took their leave, shuffling away down the paths and back across the wide lands of Skiddle Earth, singing loudly and playing their trumpets. Randolf headed out the following day, saying that he had tons of important business to catch up on after all this fooling around.

"Farewell, Mister Gabbin!" said the Wizard. "I believe we shall meet again sooner than you think, for despite your complaints, you have proven yourself quite the heroic fellow, and a fiercely loyal friend."

Bobill looked upon the kind old geezer, and with a grin, he replied, "How corny."

Randolf smiled and nodded, then turned and walked off, disappearing down the road over the distant hills, kilt flapping in the breeze.

Over the years, the Dorks would occasionally visit Bobill and destroy his home. Then they would sing really loud and leave. Bobill couldn't be happier with all that he had been through, and even though he only received one ten-thousandth of the treasure hoard, he was still as rich as a creme-filled donut.

He took to the skies in a flying machine Randolf had made for him out of grass and butter (a new design) and flew into the sunset with the wind blowing through his wig... until the machine blew up. Bobill fell to the ground and went home.

THE END

Lying in a cave, at the bottom of a cold, lightless chasm over one thousand miles away... the evil Dragon, Domard, had some rude thoughts—like getting some serious revenge on that accursed Gabbin named Bobill. He had to recover from the wounds that nearly killed him... but he would be back... and he would go nuts.

About the Author

Johann Balthasar Knörtzer is a bearded fellow who authorizes allegedly humorous, readable content. The only thing he loves more than being mysterious, is bragging about how mysterious he is.

Thank you so much for reading.

If you haven't already, please check out my social media for updates.

@johannknortzer
on Facebook & Instagram
or visit:
https://www.mythicbookspublications.com/johann

ALSO BY
JOHANN